With love to Brock Thoene— editor, friend, father.

The Mystery
of the
Yellow Hands

JAKE THOENE and LUKE THOENE

TYNDALE KIDS
TYNDALE HOUSE PUBLISHERS, INC., CAROL STREAM, ILLINOIS

BAKER STREET DETECTIVES 1

The Mystery of the Yellow Hands

Visit Tyndale's exciting Web site for kids at cool2read.com

Also see the Web site for adults at tyndale.com

TYNDALE and Tyndale's quill logo are registered trademarks of Tyndale House Publishers, Inc.

The Mystery of the Yellow Hands

Designed by Jacqueline L. Noe

Edited by Ramona Cramer Tucker

Published in 1995 by Thomas Nelson, Inc. under ISBN 0-7852-7078-7.

First printing by Tyndale House Publishers, Inc. in 2006.

Library of Congress Cataloging-in-Publication Data

Thoene, Jake.
   The mystery of the yellow hands / Jake Thoene and Luke Thoene.
      p. cm. — (The Baker Street detectives ; bk. 1)
   Summary: The three friends—Danny, Peachy, and Duff—assist Sherlock Holmes in solving the mysterious kidnapping of children in London during the 1880's.
   ISBN-13: 978-1-4143-0370-3 (hc)
   ISBN-10: 1-4143-0370-X (hc)
   [1. Kidnapping—Fiction. 2. London (England)—Fiction. 3. Mystery and detective stories.] I. Thoene, Luke. II. Title.
   PZ7.T35655Myo 2006
   [Fic]—dc22
                               2006002054

PROLOGUE

Fog shrouded the Caravaldi family home at No. 7 Trevor Place, London. Mrs. Orde, the housekeeper, and eight-year-old Emile Caravaldi were in the parlor. Mr. and Mrs. Caravaldi had gone out for the night to see the new Gilbert and Sullivan opera. Emile played on the floor with his toy soldiers while Mrs. Orde sat in a great overstuffed chair and knitted.

The town house was three stories tall. It shared walls with homes on either side, and so was closed in except for a small, high-fenced garden in the back. Brick walls lined with latticework framed this bit of open space. At the base of these frames were scraggly rosebushes, dormant in the grip of the December cold. A flat circle of brick formed the center area of the garden, upon which sat a sculpted wrought-iron table and four chairs. The family would sometimes have their afternoon tea there, but now it was too cold to sit outside.

Before the winter days had descended, Emile had converted the garden into a play battlefield, with red-painted toy soldiers and little iron cannons set up in lines around the flower bed. Atop the walls were iron spikes that curved outward away from the enclosed square. Perhaps these were intended to keep out burglars, but more than anything they kept birds from perching there.

A slight scraping noise, coming from the backyard, caused Mrs. Orde to stop knitting. She stood up to look out at the small court-yard through the French doors. With the gaslights on in the house, however, her own reflection was nearly all she could make out, except for the dim outline of the walls. Seeing nothing and hearing no more noises, she shrugged and went back to her knitting.

Emile was moving the ranks of his scarlet-coated army forward on the hearth rug as their blue-trimmed opponents retreated. Making cannon-fire noises, he brought in reinforcements to flank the enemy and cut off their retreat.

"Nanny," he said, "I need to go out and get some of my soldiers from the back. May I?"

"Of course," she replied.

Emile stood, retrieved his coat and gray-and-red-striped scarf from the rack, put them on, and opened the doors to the garden. A chilly breeze sighed in through the doorway as he collected some soldiers and a coil of rope that lay there.

"Where did that come from?" Mrs. Orde asked, pointing to the rope.

"I don't know. I found it by the wall. I think it's Daddy's," Emile explained as he shut the doors again. He sat back down but kept the rope at his side while he positioned the new men behind the retreating forces.

Little time passed before Mrs. Orde tired of her knitting and went upstairs to fetch something to read. When she headed back down to the parlor, Mrs. Orde felt a breeze blowing up the stairs.

"Emile?" she called. There was no answer.

The boy must have gone back to the garden for more toy grena-diers, she realized. Resuming her position in the chair by the fire, she opened the December 12, 1886, edition of *Strand* magazine.

Another minute passed. Still the boy did not return.

"Emile!" she scolded. She got up and walked to the open back door.

A bush nearby rustled.

"Rarrrr!" Emile screamed as he jumped out.

First startled, then angry, Mrs. Orde reprimanded him.

Emile, for his part, giggled at the success of his joke. He walked inside with yet another armful of toys.

•••

There was another witness to the scene. In the opposite corner of the garden, a figure crouched in the shadows behind a rosebush. His collar was turned up to conceal his face, from which gleamed dark, sinister eyes. His hands, clutching and scratching at the soil with impatience, were a disgusting shade of yellow, with long nails now turning black with earth.

•••

Mrs. Orde halted before stepping back into the house. She didn't know why, but something unnerved her . . . and it wasn't the silliness of a young boy. She felt eyes on her—almost as if someone were watching them. She shivered as she glanced back around the garden. But it was too dark and foggy to see anything that might be lurking in the corners.

Hurrying back inside, she shut the doors. Telling Emile to stay inside, she went to the kitchen to heat some water on the coal-fired stove.

"Your mother and father will be home soon," she explained, "and they'll want some tea." The opera Emile's parents had gone to see was in Drury Lane, and it was a long, cold carriage ride back.

•••

The shadowy figure in the garden watched as the housekeeper left the room. Then he crept slowly to the window to glare with pale eyes down on the little boy who crouched over his toy soldiers on the floor.

Slowly, stealthily, a yellow hand reached toward the door-knob. . . .

• • •

Accompanied by a sudden gust of wind, the doors from the garden flew open. Emile's head jerked up as the gas lamps flickered and danced.

His eyes widened in horror as something horrible came at him. A monster that seemed to flow in with the wind. His putrid, yellow hands were outstretched to grab!

Emile tried to scream, but he was paralyzed with fear. His mouth did not even open. He was helpless.

• • •

Hearing the rattle of the doors, Mrs. Orde marched back toward the parlor with a scolding in mind for Emile. But when she got to the hallway, she stopped in shock. A cloaked figure was clutching Emile! Black-nailed yellow hands slowly coiled a rope around the boy. When the cloaked figure looked up, Mrs. Orde staggered backward under the menacing gaze, like a bird hypnotized by a snake.

The man opened the front door and stopped. Without saying a word, he dropped a small paper-wrapped object to the floor. Then he ran, with Emile under one of his arms.

As he exited the house, Mrs. Orde followed, screaming for help. But no one was in sight as the dark carriage clattered away. She chased the carriage a short distance down the deserted street . . . until she was entirely winded.

When the black form of the coach rounded the corner and disappeared, she sank to her knees and covered her face with her hands. Emile was gone!

Mrs. Orde stumbled back to the house, her mind reeling.

It was there, in the hall, that she retrieved the only clue left behind.

One

The London thoroughfare known as the Strand was bustling with activity on the chilly afternoon. Gentlemen in silk top hats and long black coats were on their way home from important business in the City, the financial district. Ladies, wearing long skirts and bundled in fur wraps and muffs, shopped and browsed at the Lowther Arcade.

Stylish carriages, double-decker omnibuses, and hansom cabs slowly threaded through the congestion, past street-corner vendors selling bags of roasted chestnuts. The sound of the horses' hooves clattered upward from the cobblestones, bounced off the Savoy Hotel, and echoed away down to the river Thames.

Beggars dressed in ragged clothes, covered in a thick filth of coal dust and grease, sat on corners pleading with all the stately passersby for a copper or two. Shoeless children, dressed in tatters like miniature beggars, ran wild chasing each other. Chanting, they made fun of the well-to-do. These were the street urchins, children of rough parents or no parents at all.

But some of the older of them had found jobs. The Strand also rang with the calls of paperboys, eager to sell all of their copies so they could quit early and find someplace warmer.

"Extra!" they cried. "Third kidnapping in two weeks! Chief constable clueless!"

Danny Wiggins, one of the paperboys, had nearly sold out his bundle. He was thirteen and tall for his age. His dark hair with its slight curl waved in the icy breeze that swirled up Adam Street from the river.

Farther east from where Danny stood outside the Adelphi Theatre was his friend Peachy Carnehan, catching the foot traffic near the Lyceum. Peachy's real name came from his initials, P.T., but nobody now knew what they stood for. He was twelve and a fair-skinned, redheaded boy. Peachy was nearly finished with his stack of papers also.

Halfway between Peachy and Danny stood their mate Duff Bernard. Holding a gigantic heap of the *Daily Telegraph,* Duff gently swayed back and forth, waiting for either of his friends to get some more. Duff was what Danny called slow. He was fifteen and a giant, close to fourteen stone, but he was very gentle. Though he was big enough to do damage to a grown man, he would never think of it. He stood with the papers, chewing his upper lip and staring off to nowhere, oblivious to the action all around him. Like the dog of the same last name, he reminded people who knew him of a great furry, lovable animal.

"Duff," Peachy said as he walked up, "Duff, I need some more papers."

"Oh, cheerio," Duff replied, "I was just thinkin' of fish."

"Sure you were," Peachy said. "I need some more papers, though."

Just then Danny came back for more papers, too.

"Hi, Danny," Duff said. "I was just thinkin' of fish."

"Oh yeah?" Danny asked. "What about fish?"

"Oh, catchin' and eatin' . . . I'm hungry," Duff replied after a long pause.

"Well," Danny said, "we'll eat back at school after the photo. . . ." Big Ben was just striking four.

"We gotta go now!" Peachy exclaimed. "We'll be late for the picture!"

Danny and Peachy bolted down the avenue toward their street manager's location in Trafalgar Square. Duff, lagging behind under the weight of the papers, hurried to keep up.

The foreman, an unusual man with a limp and a curious sing-song voice, was a favorite of the children. They liked him for his stories of the wars in Africa, but even more for the way he told them.

"Ahhh," Mr. Mewsley sighed as the three friends came running up. "You remind me of a Zulu charge back in 1879. They came at us from all directions, and we formed into our firin' square, four ranks deep on a side, and . . ."

The boys smelled the thick smoke of the cheroots he was constantly smoking and slowed their pace. When they first met the man, Duff had described the scent of his cigars as "trash burning by the river." His habit was so constant and the tar so thick in the smoke that it stained his fingers. To any who did not know him well, Mr. Mewsley appeared a very sinister man.

"Back early I see," he said when he finished rambling about short stabbing spears and Martini rifles.

"Yes, Cap'n," Danny said. "We've pictures to take at our school."

"And then fish," Duff concluded.

"Yes . . . of course . . . fish." Mr. Mewsley smiled. "Well then, best cut along. I'll see you all tomorrow."

The boys heard him mumbling about catfish in the Nile as big as crocodiles as they trotted off down Whitehall on their way to Westminster Bridge.

●●●

Across Westminster Bridge, in the suburb of Lambeth, a notable change from the clamor of London was seen in the surroundings. The houses were old, run-down, two-story brick structures. The narrow streets wound about, yet were quieter than the richer thoroughfares.

The crooked byways were not wide enough for the larger wagons, and few people who lived there could afford carriages.

East of the river, the boys turned northward and entered Pinchin Lane. The street was frequented by other children on their way to the school. Many used it as a kind of shortcut instead of taking a main street, where they might be slowed by other traffic.

Danny, Peachy, and Duff passed a line of familiar shops. A butcher's stall stood on the left, and a foul, sulfurous-smelling tanning yard on the right, both of which were rumored to do business with the taxidermist at No. 3. It was this shop that the boys knew the best, having often stopped to look in the window at the moldy owl posed with the dead rat in its claws. They also remembered well the proprietor, since groups of children often teased him, using such names as Featherbrain, Old Blood 'n' Guts, and the Butcher's Helper. His real name was Mr. Sherman.

Mr. Sherman was a scrawny elderly man with a thin neck and sloping shoulders. He wore square-framed, blue-tinted glasses that perched near the end of his long, pointed, beaklike nose. He was bald, except for the fringe of short gray hair around the sides and back of his head, and his shiny dome was splotched with brown liver spots.

Outside the taxidermy shop this afternoon was another person they recognized easily—Mr. Sherlock Holmes, the famous private detective. His photo had recently been in all the papers regarding the mysterious case of the East End Venetian. He was famous throughout the entire city for his ability to solve crimes that baffled the Metropolitan Police.

He appeared to be there on business, for as the boys approached, they noticed him being handed the leash of a dog. The creature stood about knee-high to Mr. Holmes, and it had long fur of red, brown, and white patches. One of its uncropped ears hung down below its jaw while the other stood up. It looked like a mixture of beagle, hound, and some other unknown breed.

"Now if Toby gives you any trouble, Mr. Holmes," Sherman said, "just give him another lump of sugar. He'll follow you anywhere for that."

"Unfortunately, Sherman," Holmes replied, "I am hoping he will lead me, not follow."

"Right you are, sir, right indeed."

Just then, Mr. Sherman caught sight of the boys looking on. "Excuse me, Mr. Holmes," he said and reached inside the shop. Retrieving the great stuffed owl, he swung it by its legs like a club. "Clear off, you little beggars!"

The boys bolted up the street, stopping safely out of reach behind a pile of empty barrels. "I'm sorry," they heard Sherman continue, "but I do have trouble with those little wharf rats, always playing tricks—"

"Mr. Sherman, you are an absolute genius!" blurted Holmes. "Why had I not thought of it before?"

"Well, I . . . ," the puzzled Sherman tried to reply, but Holmes was already storming down the street toward the river, Toby lumbering eagerly at his side.

"Look for me in a week," he called. "I'll have Toby back by then."

•••

At the last bend of Pinchin Lane, Danny and the others came to Waterloo Road, where their school and indeed the only home they had was located. The school building was a converted two-story warehouse, built in 1750 and formerly used as storage for the East India Company. Its high-ceilinged rooms and great empty halls were now filled not with goods to trade but with children eager to learn. Even so, Danny remarked that he often dreamed of faraway lands, probably because of the lingering aromas of Ceylon tea and Sumatran coffee.

The outside of the structure was somewhat run-down. Its red-brick walls were chipped, and they constantly flaked red dust onto the sidewalk below. Broken windowpanes—and there were several—were boarded up from the inside. But to the children, Waterloo Road Ragged School, as it was called, was beautiful.

For the otherwise homeless young people who found shelter

there, it was more than a building to learn in. It was a sanctuary. It was the only place where they could find peace and understanding, as well as food and lodging. The people at the school not only talked about Jesus, but lived like they believed in him. They were the only adults who had ever shown kindness to many of the students in their entire lives.

The headmaster, Branford Ingram, greeted Danny, Duff, and Peachy as they ran up. "Boys! We were just about to take the picture without you. The photographer says we're losing the light."

"I'm sorry, Master Ingram," Danny said. "We had our papers to sell."

"Yes, yes, now tidy up and come along."

The boys did as they were told, tucking in shirts and straightening unruly hair. Master Ingram was a tall man, stocky and strong. He strode with his head up when he walked—not because of arrogance or pride, but out of eagerness to see the world around him. His pleasant yet rugged looks reminded the children of a military man. Indeed, he had been in the Royal Navy prior to his service at the school.

The head cook, Miss Bingham, was also present to pose for the picture. Chelsea was her Christian name, and she was a petite, pretty woman with dark curls. But all who encountered her knew that she ruled the meal service at the Ragged School and took no fooling about with her kitchen. Yet she was also a great favorite of the students for her tender heart and compassionate spirit.

The founder of the school, and many like it, was Anthony Ashley Cooper, the seventh Earl of Shaftesbury. He, too, was there for the photograph. The earl was over eighty and still tall and proud, though he walked with a cane. His head was covered with a full crop of shining white hair. His looks impressed the children and made him seem very wise, but he was not remote or unapproachable.

"Hurry up, young Wiggins," the earl called to Danny. "Gentlemen are always on time for their appointments . . . even rising young newspapermen! You, too, Carnehan and Bernard!" His good-natured teasing made the whole assembly laugh, from the front rank of sprats on up to the older boys who stood on the top step in back.

There was not a day when the earl was not seen at one of the schools talking or playing with some of the children, and for that, they loved him. A grandfather to many, he was still treated with immense respect. Not a person, adult or child, called him anything other than "m' lord."

When the earl strolled up and took his place on the steps before the front doors of the school, the entire group fell silent. From his spot in the highest row, Danny sighed with relief that they had made it in time.

The photographer was a Turkish man, wearing a black suit, white gloves, and a red fez on the top of his head. Part of his bulky equipment was tied to the top of a small white donkey that stood patiently waiting. Also tied to the donkey, and acting anything but patient, was a brown monkey that chattered when anyone besides his master approached too closely.

Mounted on a large wooden tripod was an enormous folding camera. A stack of wooden photographic plates was heaped on the ground nearby. The photographer gazed at his selected instrument for a moment, then slipped off a small round cover and peered through the open back of the Marion and Company panoramic camera. Danny was fascinated by its brass lens and fittings and its expanse of leather bellows.

Pulling a hood over his head and the back of the camera, the photographer adjusted a whole series of knobs and dials. Some knobs angled the lens up or down, and a dial pulled the entire camera in and out like an accordion. When all was set, he rose from the hood, took a plate from the stack on the ground, and in heavily accented and clipped English, directed the group to hold still and not move.

The smell from the flash powder was overpowering to the boys. But the ignition of the silvery dust also gave off an impressive display of thick, yellow-tinted smoke and a whooshing explosion, which pleased them very much.

●●●

The photograph successfully concluded, the boys of Waterloo Road Ragged School headed to the dining hall for their evening meal. Master Ingram said a prayer of thanks, and the children lined up to get their dinners. Duff got his plate, immediately found his seat, and dug into a large portion of mutton stew.

"Not fish," Peachy observed as he sat down, "but the way Duff is going at it, it must be good."

"It's always good," Danny said, "if Miss Bingham makes it."

"No," Duff managed through a mouthful of stew. "It's always good if I like it."

Danny and Peachy laughed at this, and Duff joined in, not really knowing what they were laughing at.

For a time the chatter and jostle always present in a group of a hundred young boys fell silent. The clink of spoons replaced conversation as the serious matter of eating took all concentration. The sounds of silverware clanking were punctuated by an occasional slurp, but the children whispered even when they asked for the salt.

When the meal was coming to an end, the babble gradually resumed its full strength, once again filling the hall with a constant hum. Silence again dropped abruptly over the crowd when Sherlock Holmes, with Toby on a leash, unexpectedly entered the room with the earl by his side.

The lean, angular detective paused at the doors and removed his tall silk hat. He peered around the room, giving each table a severe study as if he were angry. All were quiet. All stared back at him. Even the handful of the youngest boys, who did not know Holmes by sight, were instantly shushed when they tried to ask who he was.

With Toby meandering at his side, Mr. Holmes strode along the heads of the tables, pulling at the fingers of his gloves as he removed them. He appeared to be searching for someone in particular. He glanced at every young face in turn until he happened upon the ones he wanted. Danny wondered which of the children had done something so wrong that a distinguished investigator would bring a dog to catch the culprit.

When Holmes stopped beside Danny's table, Duff continued to slurp his stew. Danny swallowed hard also, but he had no further interest in supper.

The detective walked up the length of the table to where the three friends sat and spoke to them. "I am Sherlock Holmes," he said to Peachy. "Who is in charge here?"

Peachy's jaw dropped, and he quickly pointed at Danny. Returning a look of anger and dismay at Peachy's betrayal, Danny turned to face Holmes. Could the taxidermist, Mr. Sherman, somehow have convinced Holmes to arrest them? What was this all about?

"Y-yes, sir?" Danny stammered. "What did I . . . that is, we, do?"

"No, no, no, my dear boy, you are not in trouble. I came here for your help."

"You did?" Danny cleared his throat to cover up the fact that his voice had squeaked. "You did?" he repeated with extra emphasis to show his mates that he was not really startled almost out of his wits.

"Yes," Holmes replied. "Your lordship," he addressed the earl, who had followed the detective to the table, "I believe these are the three we were discussing. I wonder if I might have a few moments of time alone with the gentlemen?"

The earl nodded his agreement and gave a sign of assent to the equally stunned Master Ingram. The headmaster jumped up from where he sat beside Miss Bingham and led the way out of the dining hall to his private office. Duff, who was still eating, mopped up the last of the gravy with a crust of bread, then followed the group out.

"I've come on important business," Mr. Holmes explained. "As you may have heard, there have been three kidnappings in the past two weeks. The police are as baffled as your *Daily Telegraph* headlines have declared."

Danny wondered how he knew that they were paperboys, much less for which paper they worked.

"What I am about to tell you has not been revealed to the public and must remain in strictest confidence. Agreed?"

Overwhelmed at the thought that Sherlock Holmes was about to share a secret with them, Danny and Peachy nodded solemnly, and Duff, imitating them, did likewise.

"In each case, a stone is dropped, wrapped in a note that reads *Wait for the letter*. Then a letter arrives at the missing child's house exactly two days later. The letter states that the child will not be hurt unless the family fails to meet the modest demands. It goes on to ask for one hundred pounds."

Danny looked at the headmaster and the earl, hoping for some clues as to where this discussion was leading. But their expressions were as baffled as his own. Duff, meanwhile, scratched Toby's ears, and the dog wagged his tail appreciatively.

"Each letter is accompanied by a photograph," Holmes continued, "showing that the child is still alive, but held in a cage suspended above the ground. The room appears dark and damp, with some crates in the background. In two of the photos, a coil of rope lies next to the cage."

Danny noticed that the earl, with his particular concern for children, looked almost in pain when he heard about the dreadful scenes.

"I fear for the safety of these children because the first two ransoms were not collected," Holmes explained. He paused as if in deep thought before continuing. "It is strange because in the first case, the father, an official at the French embassy, followed the instructions completely. He told no one until the allotted time had passed. But no one appeared to collect the money, and his child was not returned."

Danny and Peachy exchanged a puzzled look. This was all exciting information, but what did it have to do with them? Duff appeared not to be listening at all. He was sitting on the floor, still scratching Toby behind the ears.

"Scotland Yard ruined the second attempt to pay the ransom because of their obvious presence on the scene. So we will never know whether the kidnappers intended to return that child or not. The third set of parents, a family named Caravaldi, came to me."

"I beg your pardon, sir," Peachy said, "but why tell us? I mean, you want us to get kidnapped, too?"

"No, no. This afternoon on Pinchin Lane, I was inspired by something said by my friend, the owner of Toby here. In fact, it's what he called you. Not very complimentary perhaps. I believe the expression was 'wharf rats.'"

"What? You mean old Featherbrain?" Peachy said hotly, despite Danny's efforts to quiet him down. "He wouldn't know a wharf rat if he stuffed one himself. Where does he get off—?"

"Ahhh," Holmes interrupted, "but you are. And there's money in it for you if you can be."

When Peachy got abruptly silent and attentive, Danny gave a grin. His friend's feelings were easily soothed at the mention of money.

"You see," Holmes continued, "from the amount of moisture evident on the wall shown in the photograph, it's obvious that the kidnapped children are being held somewhere by the river. The rope is coiled in a distinctive nautical style, suggesting a wharf or dock area, as do the crates in the background. All of these clues indicate the waterfront, along which you can move more freely and unnoticed than I. I might track the culprits to their lair with the aid of Toby here."

Toby and Duff both turned their faces toward Holmes.

"But my appearance in an area might cause the kidnappers to move the children elsewhere, or worse," Holmes added. "I must have more information before we swoop down on them."

Danny then understood what it was he and Peachy and Duff were to do for Mr. Holmes. "You want us to investigate around the docks and the shipping warehouses."

"No!" Holmes said sharply. "I merely want you to observe. Walk past the riverfront, paying attention to anything out of the ordinary, and report back to me whatever you see. Are we agreed? It's worth a shilling for each of you."

"Done!" Danny and Peachy said almost in unison.

Duff smiled.

Toby barked happily, bouncing up and down on his stubby front legs.

Two

The next day the sharp smells of charcoal smoke and steaming horse dung thickened the crisp morning air. The clopping of the heavy iron shoes of the draft horses rang like a thousand clocks, ticking away the morning on the cobblestones south of London Bridge.

On the sidewalk, a soiled and tired crowd of workingmen flowed as slowly and silently as oil. Many had worked since midnight, stocking the meat markets and vegetable stalls, and were now on their way home to sleep. Danny, Duff, and Peachy had to fight against the current of surly pedestrians heading upstream.

Hats of many shapes and colors blocked their view. "What can you see, Duff?" Danny asked, craning his neck.

"Heads," Duff replied simply.

"No, silly," Peachy corrected. "He means, can you see the building yet?"

Duff looked puzzled.

Peachy reached up and tapped him hard on the head. "The big burned-out building with the red smoky letters at the top!"

"'Course! There it is." Duff pointed, stretching out a huge hand and knocking the bowler hat off of a man in front of him.

The man turned, scowling, and opened his mouth for an angry retort.

Danny smiled as the man's eyes took in Duff. They widened, evidently at Duff's size. Then the man promptly shut his mouth.

Duff retrieved the derby with a bashful apology.

Peachy just shook his head.

When they reached the river, at the end of the bridge, the boys turned off and descended the gray granite stairs to the level of the water. The stone steps were smooth and worn down in the middle from centuries of foot traffic. At the bottom the three turned east, ducking under the bridge and heading along the river.

Captain Garrett's Chandlery had been built along the Thames in the year 1830. John Garrett had been a seafaring man, whose business in spare rigging and ships' stores had boomed, despite the peculiar building housing it. Captain Garrett, though land-bound after losing an arm in the wars with the French, had wanted everything shipshape and Bristol fashion. So he'd constructed his headquarters with portholes for windows and topped it with the rigging of a three-masted ship of the line.

At the zenith of his trade, Captain Garrett had equipped ships traveling all the oceans of the world. But greed got the better of him, and he was hanged for piracy. Shortly after his death, the building burned. Some said that the vengeful ghost of the captain himself had set the torch. Many people still regarded the gutted heap of bricks as an evil place.

Danny considered the abandoned building with apprehension. Despite his agreement to Peachy's suggestion, Danny thought that Captain Garrett's was a very creepy spot indeed.

Peachy nodded toward the building. "See. Mr. Holmes said for us to be on the lookout for anything suspicious, and there can't be nothing more suspicious in all of south London than old Garrett's place."

The three friends studied the odd round windows. Each broken-out porthole was topped with streaks of scorch marks that reached up like spikes of black hair. It made the wall resemble row upon row of screaming heads.

"Right, then," Danny said slowly.

He really wanted to back out, but as the leader of the group—now even addressed that way by Sherlock Holmes himself—he felt stuck. He also considered sending Peachy, since this exploration had been his idea, but the thought seemed cowardly.

"Right, then," he repeated. "This is what we'll do. Peachy, you and I'll go together to check the inside, and Duff, you watch the outside."

Danny paused and spoke very deliberately so Duff would be clear. "Give us a warning in case anybody comes. . . ."

Peachy objected. "Now hang on there a minute, mate."

"What's the matter?" Danny asked Peachy.

Peachy blushed. "I ain't scared of no kidnappers or nothing."

Danny spread out his hands. "Nobody said you were."

"What I meant was, I just thought there was a lot of ground to cover," Peachy explained. "One of us should look around out here."

It was somehow a relief to find that Peachy was also nervous about going in the chandlery building. Danny felt better about his own fears. He looked out at the barges going about their business on the river and across the Thames to where the great dome of St. Paul's Cathedral dominated the skyline. It all looked very commonplace and normal.

"Fair enough," Danny said with a shrug. "If I see anything strange, I'll come tell you, and if you blokes see anything funny, then you better come tell me. All right?"

"Done." Peachy turned and walked off toward the river.

Duff began to follow, then stopped, taking a step back toward Danny. The large boy looked confused.

"It's all right, Duff," Danny said. "Go on with him. But be quick about it. We've got to pick up our papers by noon."

"Fair enough," Duff replied, smiling. Then he trotted off to catch up with Peachy.

•••

Peachy walked down to the docks, looking for something else that would qualify as suspicious. The river water lapped softly against the old pilings that lined the edge of the wharf. He crouched down by some empty barrels to study the scene along the river. The chilly air heightened the color in his cheeks, and his breath rose in a steamy cloud.

At the edge of the water sat the rotting wooden corpse of what had once been a river schooner. Now dismasted, streaked with rust stains, and coated with grime, the hull was little more than a roost for seagulls. Still connected to the pilings by heavy cables and a plank walkway, the boat sat on the mud. Tilted by low tide, it leaned away from the dock, as if wishing it could follow the retreating waters down to the sea.

The flat expanse of deck, long since scavenged of anything valuable, was relieved only by a small cabin at the stern and a thick hatch cover toward the bow.

Peachy sighed. Detective work was not turning out to be as exciting as he had imagined it would be. And it was a little lonely, too.

He squinted through a porthole, trying to look past years of accumulated coal soot and bird droppings. And then . . . something moved inside the boat!

Peachy's heart pounded. He scrambled in back of the barrels and flattened himself in order to spy on the ship without being seen.

Cautiously he peered around a wooden keg that boasted IMPERIAL SARDINES ARE THE BEST IN THE WORLD! From a distance of two inches, the empty barrel still had the aroma of its former occupants.

Peachy held his breath and waited . . . for what felt like a long time.

But he could see no further movement from the ship. No noises came from it either.

Soon Peachy's arms and legs became stiff from the cold and the awkward position. So stiff, in fact, that he could scarcely move.

Suddenly heavy footsteps came up behind him, rattling the dock.

Peachy tried to jump up, collided with the sardine drum, and landed awkwardly in a heap.

Big feet stood just in front of him.

"I didn't mean to scare ya, Peachy," Duff's voice said. He chuckled.

"Shhh, get down!" Peachy said urgently, anxious to cover his embarrassment. "I saw something moving inside the cabin."

Duff scrambled for cover behind the barrels.

Just as he did so, both boys heard an injured cry from the hulk.

"Ouch! You grotty little nipper!" an infuriated voice shouted. "So you want to be a tough guy, huh? We'll see about that!" A man's angry red face, contorted with pain, passed by the grimy window. It disappeared from view momentarily, heading toward the stern, then returned by the opening again. "Come here, you little brat! I'll teach you! I'll wrap you up tighter than a hangman's noose!"

The protesting shriek of little-used hinges caused the heads of the two boys to pivot sharply toward the hatch cover. A hairy hand emerged from the hold, pushing the thick deck plate upward. The lid resisted being opened. Then a pair of burly arms appeared from below, flinging the hatch cover back with a crash.

The decaying hull boomed from the impact like a giant wooden drum, and the lines binding the ship to the shore rattled.

"What's all this racket then?" demanded a rough bass voice. Out of the hatchway climbed a heavyset man, short but with a big belly. He had a tangle of black beard that reached to his chest, but the hair on his head was thin and scraggly. He stalked down the deck and into the cabin. "Ye be careful with him! He'll fetch me a pretty penny, but he's got to be unharmed!"

Peachy spun around, thinking fast. "Duff," he whispered urgently, "go quick while they're busy! Go get Danny! Tell him we found the kidnappers!"

Duff's eyes bulged, his mouth open wide. "Kidnappers! I'll go get Danny." He jumped to his feet and ran off, almost knocking several barrels into the river.

Peachy watched to see that no one on the ship had noticed Duff's departure. Then he slid up close to the barrels to peek through again.

The case was as good as solved!

●●●

"Danny! Danny, come quick!" Duff called. His stumbling feet kicked up clouds of antique dust and ancient ash. The cinders swirled into his nose and throat and blinded his eyes. "Danny, where are you?"

Duff rubbed his face to clear his vision, then had to wait for his eyes to adjust to the darkness of the burned-out shell of Garrett's Chandlery. "Dannnyyy," he cried.

Why did Danny not answer? And Peachy had said to bring him back right away!

"Duff, I'm up here," Danny's voice finally answered. His words seemed to float down from somewhere.

"Where?" Duff searched the dark corners overhead, as if expecting to find Danny flying around the room. The fire that had destroyed the building had left the walls standing but had burned right up through the roof. Duff could see daylight at the very top of the structure. Looking straight up made him dizzy.

"Stay there. I'm coming," Danny called. Then his face appeared, over the railing of a platform two levels above Duff. "I'm up here. I've been clear to the top. There's nothing. Even rats would fall through what's left of the floors."

Duff began to smile. "Huh."

"No place for kidnappers at all," Danny concluded, coming down a step. "It could all collapse any minute."

Kidnappers! Now Duff remembered the important news! "Kidnappers! Danny! Peachy says come quick! The kidnappers are on a boat!"

"What? He found them? I'll be right there!"

At that instant there was a sharp crack, followed by a ponderous groaning. The charred timbers supporting the stairs and what remained of the floors popped and squealed as if Captain Garrett's building were a ship in the midst of a hurricane.

Danny staggered and grabbed for the railing as the landing on which he stood tilted away from the wall. His feet went out from under him, and he fell and rolled toward the drop-off. He caught hold of a post before almost plunging over the edge into forty feet of air.

"Danny!" Duff yelled as he got a heap of falling ashes and dust in his face. Boards and bricks rained around him, striking him on the head and shoulders. Blinded, he threw up his arms to protect himself and stumbled away from the opening. Choking and coughing, he sputtered out a mouthful of white grit, all the while calling for Danny.

When the hail of bricks and lumber stopped and the creaking noises slowed, Duff peered upward again through squinted eyes.

Danny was still hanging on the edge of the chasm, but only barely. The full weight of his body hung over the drop, and the post to which he clung was shaking with the tension.

"Duff," Danny called softly, "go get help."

"I'll help you," Duff said.

"No. It isn't safe for you either."

But Duff had seen what the truth was: Danny could not hang on more than another minute. His grip might fail, or the beam could pull loose. There was no time to get anyone else. It was up to Duff.

The stairs leaned out from the wall, but Duff took the treads two at a time, hurrying toward Danny. When a timber creaked, he stopped, but only for a moment. Placing each step over the few brick supports that projected from the wall, he moved quickly but carefully.

When he reached the level where Danny hung suspended, he dropped to his knees. Laying down flat, Duff stretched out to his full length. "It's all right. I'm almost there." Hooking the toes of his boots in the gap between the wall and the platform, he scooted, headfirst, down the inclined floor. He reached out his hands toward his friend.

Danny's feet swung in midair as he grasped the post with both hands. "I can't let go to grab on to you. Go back, Duff. Save yourself."

"It's goin' to be all right." Duff lifted his feet until only a bare fraction of an inch of shoe leather kept him above the fall. "There," he said with satisfaction. "Now I can grab you."

The extra inch gave him enough room to reach out and grasp Danny's jacket by the shoulders. "Now I'll pull you up to me," he said matter-of-factly. "Here we go. Catch hold of my back and climb me like a ladder."

The remaining props cracked and whined a warning. There was no time to waste! Danny scrambled up Duff's back and reached the brick wall. He put all his weight on Duff's feet, forcing the toes into the crack. "Hurry!" he urged. "Get up here quick!"

As soon as both boys were on the stairs, they vaulted down from landing to landing until they reached the ground floor.

Just then the platform groaned again, swaying like a mast in a high wind. Then it toppled toward the boys.

"Look out!" Danny yelled. He and Duff jumped through the opening and outside Garrett's Chandlery as the stairs collapsed with a thundering roar and an explosion of dust.

Danny and Duff slumped to the pavement, covered in grime and ashes. "Thanks, mate," Danny said. "You saved my hide for certain that time. What was it again you came after me for?"

Both boys' eyes widened, and their heads snapped around toward each other. "Peachy!" they shouted as one voice. "Kidnappers!"

•••

Peachy impatiently glanced over his shoulder for the hundredth time. Where were Duff and Danny? From the bumping and jostling noises coming from the ship, it seemed a certainty that something was about to happen. But what?

The door to the ship's cabin flew open. Out came the fat bearded man, followed by the other man Peachy had glimpsed through the porthole. The skinny second bloke had a roll of carpet slung over his shoulder.

"Take him to the cellar, and be quick about it," the bearded man ordered.

Take him to the cellar?! Someone was rolled up in that rug, and they were taking him to a basement, just as Sherlock Holmes had deduced! Peachy's anger rose at the thought of a poor, helpless boy stuffed inside a moth-eaten piece of carpet. His heartbeat rose with his indignation.

The gangling accomplice struggled with his burden as he carried the carpet toward the ship's gunwale, then onto the plank. The coil of rug bounced up and down on his shoulder, and its unwilling occupant emitted muffled complaining noises that sounded almost like growls. The carpet kicked up and down, and Peachy silently applauded the captive boy's efforts to free himself. The kidnapper balanced awkwardly on the narrow walkway, stopping twice to readjust the load.

"That's right, lad," Peachy muttered. "Don't make it easy for them."

Peachy readied himself behind the barrels. What could he do to stop this? he wondered. He searched the dock one last time and shot a silent prayer heavenward. *God, help me find something useful.* He spotted a broken cart, a two-foot length of rope, but nothing he could use as a weapon.

Could he push the heap of barrels over on the man? Possibly, but the fall to the mud below might injure the one Peachy was trying to save.

Peachy edged closer, but his foot was hung up on something behind one of the barrels. Then he saw. . . .

There it was, an answer to his prayers, in plain sight on the ground. A discarded fisherman's gaff, solid oak from end to end and capped with a heavy metal, spiked hook on the top. Peachy's hands clenched the shaft, and he judged the nearness of the approaching footsteps.

The man reached the dock and turned, heading straight for Peachy's hiding place. Armed with the Lord and a mighty big stick, Peachy's Irish blood began to boil.

Several feet from the barrels, the scoundrel's fate was already sealed. Peachy jumped to his feet, ready for battle. He swung his weapon through the air. It made a rushing *whoosh*, as of a great windstorm. Startled by the noise and the sudden appearance of a blow coming toward him, the man dropped his cargo onto the dock.

Crack! The man's head was no match for Peachy's improvised club, and the man hit the planks. His knees crumpled to the pier, and his stomach followed. His chin and outstretched arms bounced awkwardly off the pavement.

The rug twisted and squirmed, kicking even harder to be let free. Peachy was overwhelmed with joy at the success of his rescue. The spiral of carpet broke open, its hostage freed.

Out rushed a vicious, thickset, red-coated bulldog. It foamed at the mouth, snapped at the air and the leg of the man lying on the ground, then ran off toward London Bridge.

Peachy stood, feeling stupid, and watched the dog's retreat. He heard the slam of the cabin door again.

"Ye little piece of sewage!" a violent voice exclaimed. "That's me prize fighting dog!"

Peachy turned just in time to see the large bearded man charging up the plank . . . right toward him!

Peachy dropped his gaff and fled. Turning the corner of the shipyard between the dock and the burned-out building, Peachy collided head-on with two more people. Instantly his fists were flying, as were his feet.

Several punches and kicks landed before he realized he recognized the shouts of greeting and pain as coming from Danny and Duff.

As the boys untangled themselves from a heap on the ground, not far behind them they heard, "Come back here, ye shark bait. I'll drown ye! So help me, I will! I'll drown ye!"

Three

The three friends ran down Tooley Street toward London Bridge Station. When they neared the railway terminal, they ducked inside to lose their pursuer. The station was swarming with travelers on their way to the countryside or to the seacoast. The constant arrivals and departures of the coal-fired locomotives had blackened the high ceiling with thick soot.

The crowded confusion of the station allowed Danny, Peachy, and Duff to stop for a few moments and catch their breath.

"Blimey," Danny said. "We really bungled that one."

"Yeah," Peachy agreed. "Fine lot of detectives we turned out to be. That fat bearded beast could have killed us!"

"Um," Duff interrupted, pulling on Peachy's sleeve, "do you mean the man on the ship?"

"Yes, Duff," Danny said patiently. "The one who chased us."

"Well . . . ," Duff said slowly, raising his long arm to shoulder level and pointing across the train station to the entrance. "There he is now."

Danny and Peachy spun around. Sure enough, the man was walking slowly, but with angry determination, right toward them. In his hand he had a length of rope.

"Run!" Danny exclaimed, and the three bolted out onto St. Thomas Street.

"This way!" Peachy yelled, though he did not know exactly where he was leading them. First south on Weston Street, then east on Snowsfields, then south again on Bermondsey. On Bermondsey, they scampered past a man leading a heavily loaded donkey. It was the Turkish photographer who had taken their picture, but the boys had neither breath nor time to greet the man.

As they headed east on White's Grade, the road curved around to the north. By now, the boys had taken so many turns that they knew for certain no one could have followed.

"Well," Peachy panted through gasping breaths, "looks like we lost him."

"No," said Duff, "I think we lost us. I've never been here before."

Peachy realized with a jolt that indeed they were far out of place. The houses in the neighborhood in which they found themselves were modest but definitely well above the district around the school. These were the homes of respectable people, wage earners, to be sure, but higher in standing than the costermongers and street vendors.

The houses were faced with white plaster finished to look like stone, with fronts of fake stone pillars or wrought iron. It was a neighborhood of families who were not wealthy, but well-off. Peachy remarked that the homes belonged to people who were "putting on airs."

All the houses looked identical—three stories high, with two windows on each level. Wrought-iron railings, painted black, with lumpy wrought-iron pineapples on every third post, connected all the buildings. Beside each entryway was an opening with stairs going down a flight to the cellars or kitchens. Only the house number on the square brass plate attached to the left side of each door gave variety.

No. 21, the house where they had stopped running, had a black crepe sash draped over the door, a sign that a member of the family had recently died. Someone had drawn curtains across the inside of the windows, shutting the house off from the street and the rest of the outside world.

Just then, a playful gust of wind swirled past, snatching Duff's ragged tweed cap off his head. The breeze spun the cap down the steps leading toward the cellar door. Duff rattled the gate that enclosed the stairwell but found it locked.

All three boys just stared down at the cap. "More bad luck," Peachy said.

"I'll get it," Danny volunteered. "Be back in a minute."

•••

Danny climbed over the fence and descended the stairs. When he reached the bottom, he paused, then looked up and smiled. "Easy," he called up to his friends, then disappeared from their sight to retrieve the cap.

At that moment, the door behind him swung open. Danny swiveled to face a young girl about his age.

The girl was pretty. She had brown eyes, and the tight ringlets of her dark hair were gathered back from her face. They just touched her neck in the back. When she smiled, she had perfect teeth, gleaming white.

Danny could feel his face turning red.

"Hello," the girl said to Danny. "My name is Clair. You came after your hat?" She picked up the cap and extended it toward Danny.

But Danny couldn't move. Feeling dumb and tongue-tied, he just stared at her.

"Do you speak English?" she teased. "I said my name is Clair. What's yours?"

"Uh, Danny," he replied at last. "My mate's cap . . . you see . . . the wind . . . you understand?"

"Oh yes," she replied, "that's quite all right."

"Well then, I'll be going," he concluded lamely and began to climb the stairs.

"No, wait," she said, stopping him.

Danny froze. Was this Clair going to call the law and have him arrested for trespassing?

"You're not from around here, are you?" she asked. "I should like to meet your friend, if I may."

•••

When the door opened suddenly, Peachy and Duff ran. They didn't know who or what was coming out!

They weren't usually so jumpy but had become so because of the recent experience with the bearded man. Sprinting to the corner, they grabbed on to the tall iron post of a streetlamp. Their momentum spun them around.

Any moment they expected to hear Danny start yelling and to see a big man carry him out by the collar.

"What'll we do?" Duff said anxiously, shaking Peachy's shoulder.

"I don't know. Be quiet and let me think!"

As Peachy and Duff waited, the photographer and the donkey turned the corner behind them.

"Cor!" Peachy said. "It's like we're being chased everywhere we go!"

"More bad luck," Duff said, imitating Peachy's words from earlier.

But as the Turkish man passed by with a tip of his red fez and a polite "Good morning," Peachy saw Danny emerge from the stairwell and advance up the street by the side of a beautiful young woman.

"A girl," Peachy gasped. "And a stunner! Why couldn't I have gotten the cap?"

"More bad luck," Duff agreed.

"Top of the morning, Danny," Peachy called, putting on the manners of a swell to impress the girl. "Who might this lovely lady be?"

"This is Clair," Danny answered without much enthusiasm.

He sounded a bit embarrassed. As he and Clair drew closer,

Danny introduced them. "Clair, this is Peachy, and the strapping great chap behind him is our mate Duff. It's him has lost his cap."

Duff's attention was occupied elsewhere. He watched the man with the monkey unpack a camera and unfold a tripod. Duff smiled when the monkey chattered.

"Well, Duff," Clair said, "here is your cap back."

Suddenly Duff turned toward the girl. His smile turned to a look of serious concentration, and he gravely accepted the cap. To the amazement of his friends, he gave a deep graceful bow to Clair, sweeping the ragged tweed cap across his body before popping it neatly back on his head.

"Cor!" Peachy muttered. "Where'd he learn a trick like that?"

"So what brings you here?" Clair asked, amused by the obvious attention of the three admirers.

"We were running . . . ," Danny started.

"We are on important business for Mr. Sherlock Holmes," Peachy corrected. "No doubt you've heard of him. Detective chap."

"How amazing!" she said. "Certainly I know Mr. Holmes. My father is Inspector Jonathan Avery of Scotland Yard. What case of Mr. Holmes's are you working on?"

Peachy's jaw dropped, and he lost the thread of his important mission, right in midthought. "Well, we've . . . uh . . . we've got to get back to it, whatever it is we've got to do. Nice to meet you, though."

"Peachy," Danny said, gathering up the reins of command, "that's not very nice after you've just met the girl. Actually we are helping in the matter of the strange kidnappings, but we're not supposed to talk about it."

"What awful crimes! But what an interesting coincidence! My father is also investigating that case. I am hopeful that it will help him to be so involved in his work. Last spring, you see, my mother . . ." Clair waved her hand at the drawn curtains and the black ribbon over the door.

A pained glance swept between Danny and Peachy. Yes, they knew all about death. So did all the children at the Waterloo Road Ragged School.

Just then the smiling photographer joined the group. He removed his fez with a white-gloved hand and offered Clair a bow even deeper than Duff's.

"Excuse me, dear miss," he said with his heavy accent. "Would you perhaps like to have your picture taken on the donkey with the monkey? Most charming, and only a shilling. These young men can vouch for my work. Most excellent, I assure you."

"Why, I believe I will," she said. "It might cheer my father up."

"It will cost only a shilling, and you do not have to pay me until I return it for your approval."

Clair climbed on the donkey, assisted by the gloved hand of the polite little man. The monkey squeaked and squealed, making the boys laugh. It ran up Clair's arm, perched on top of her head, then ran down the other arm and out on the donkey's head.

Duff laughed so hard and so loudly that the windows in the neighborhood rattled.

After the photo was taken, the photographer packed up his gear and went on his way, and the friends began to talk again in front of Clair's home.

"Will a silly photo like that cheer your father?" Danny asked.

"Oh, I do hope so! My mother passed away nearly six months ago. I miss her greatly, but I fear for my father. Dear Papa has been so sad. His work has suffered, and anything I can do to help him, I will."

The group was silent awhile.

"I lost both my parents," Peachy said at last. "It was in Africa, it was. I don't even remember what they looked like or what happened to them. I just know that I made it back to England somehow, but it took a long time. That's how I ended up in an orphanage. An awful place!"

"How very strange! Dear Papa was in Africa with the army. Are you staying in the orphanage now?"

"Bless you, no! I ran away from that place. I was dipping pockets on the Strand when I met Danny and Duff. They were selling papers, and they told me about the Ragged School."

"The school begun by that dear earl?"

"The Earl of Shaftesbury. That's right. We stay there, learn there, eat there. It's nice. Now I sell papers with Danny and Duff here. I don't make as much as when I was pulling, but the Ragged School, they gave me what they call a conscience."

He looked at Danny and Duff and smiled. The people at the Ragged School had given all three of them more than that. They'd told the boys stories that had not only given them consciences, but changed their hearts, too. But Peachy knew that sometimes people outside the school didn't understand, so he decided to leave it at that, for now.

"Having a conscience means I'd feel bad if I took anything that wasn't mine," Peachy added.

A man's voice from inside Clair's home rang out. "Clair? Where are you?"

"That's my father," Clair said. She seemed to study their tattered clothes and grimy faces, as if seeing the condition of her new friends for the first time. "I'd better go in," she said, looking down.

Danny caught on at once. "Do go in, miss," he offered. "Wouldn't be right for you to be found speaking with the likes of us."

Clair gave him a grateful smile. "Do come again. When my father is feeling better, I know he'll be glad to meet you. He's really very nice."

With that she was gone.

Peachy reminded Duff and Danny that they needed to hurry or they would be late for work. Then he gave his conclusion about the chance meeting. "Come again, she says. Not likely! This neighborhood . . . and her old man a crusher besides."

But Danny raised an eyebrow, as if he might be thinking differently.

•••

The clanking of the brass door knocker sounded like the blows of a blacksmith's hammer as it rapped hard against the outside door of

221B Baker Street. Peachy's soiled fingers grasped the shiny metal as he waited expectantly for a response.

Embarrassed at their lack of success in the investigating business, Danny and Peachy were not eager to recount their failure to the master sleuth. They had drawn straws to see who would knock at the door, and Peachy had lost. The truth was that Duff was completely unconcerned about the detective's reaction, but the luck of the draw made Peachy the choice.

"Mr. Holmes!" Peachy yelled up to the second story. When no answer was forthcoming, Peachy asked, "Are you sure this is it, Danny? Could be we've come to the wrong digs."

"Of course it is. It's the only 221B, isn't it?" Danny replied sarcastically.

Duff stopped chewing his lip, which he always did when in deep thought, and looked up. "Maybe he's not home."

"That's it!" Peachy agreed, unable to keep the relief out of his voice. "Come on then. Let's clear off."

"What is all the shouting about?" A second-story window swung open, crashing into an empty clay vase that in summer would have held a living plant. The flowerpot went sailing to the ground, struck the sidewalk to the right of the doorway, and smashed into thousands of bits.

The three friends jumped at the explosion. Their heads snapped upward to find a dressing-gown-clad Sherlock Holmes staring back at them. Unsure how to recover from the fall of the clay vase, the boys said nothing.

"Ah! It's you, my wharf rats," Holmes said with a happy smirk. It was as if he did not notice the pot's demise at all. "Come up, come up! Bring me your report."

"Yes, sir," Danny replied. The shutters crashed together again, and Danny turned to look at his companions. Peachy shrugged. It was plain that Mr. Holmes was a little crazy already. What would he be like if he became angry? While Peachy and Danny hesitated, Duff was already pushing into the entrance.

The wide black door opened into a small but elegant entryway, leading to a flight of stairs. With a slam of the front door and the banging of three pairs of booted feet, the boys ran past a small mahogany table on which Holmes's top hat and gloves were lying.

A door at the end of the entryway opened, and they were confronted by the housekeeper, Mrs. Hudson. She was small but plump, with white hair pulled back in a bun, and she wore a blue apron. "Boys! Boys! Don't run in the house."

"We have official business with Mr. Sherlock Holmes," Peachy said nervously.

Mrs. Hudson, looking very stern with her hands on her hips, stood blocking the stairway. "Oh no, you don't. Not until you go back down and take off those filthy boots!" Her voice ended on a high squeaking note.

"Mrs. Hudson," Holmes snapped from the landing one flight up, "pray do not detain my employees! May I introduce my own company of irregular troops, my wharf-rat sleuths, none other than the Baker Street Brigade."

"Oh, dear," the housekeeper said, rolling her eyes and standing to the side. "Getting young boys to do your dirty work now, I see."

"Thank you, Mrs. Hudson. That will be all now," Holmes said sharply. "Come up, Wiggins. Bring the company to my study."

Danny, Peachy, and Duff scurried past Mrs. Hudson up the stairs and into the study, overlooking Baker Street.

"Come in," Holmes welcomed. "Sit down and tell me what you've found."

"We found this old suspicious building—," Danny began, only to be interrupted by Peachy.

"But first, I was at the dock with Duff, and I saw these kidnappers. Then I sent Duff to get Danny and—"

"And the floor fell, and I saved Danny," Duff added.

"Then this fat bearded captain showed up, and he said that his prisoner was worth a lot of money. And a sailor had him rolled in a carpet, and he was kicking," Peachy continued.

Holmes scooted forward to the edge of his seat. He steepled his fingers together and licked his lips. "And then what?"

Danny tried again. "The bloke with the carpet was coming down the dock, so Peachy jumped up and knocked him cold with a gaff."

Holmes's shoulders began to shake. He gave a short burst of a laugh, much like the bark of a dog, and his left eye twitched. "Go on."

"The sailor dropped the rug, and this mean dog that was in it ran away. Then we ran away, too, because the large chap said he would drown us," Danny finished, and suddenly the room seemed very still. "What do you think?" he asked softly.

Holmes burst into laughter. "Ha! Did you say a dog? Ha! Mrs. Hudson, Mrs. Hudson! Come quick. These boys stopped a dognapper with a boat hook." He subsided into repressive chuckles, punctuated by an occasional shouted "Ha!"

Duff broke into laughter along with Holmes, but Peachy's pride was smashed. His pale cheeks turned as red as the velvet cushions on the sofa.

Danny ground his teeth and clenched and unclenched his fists. Fighting back a lump in his throat, he wondered what Sherlock Holmes, the greatest detective of all time, must think about them now.

After another minute, Holmes calmed down. All eyes were upon him, waiting for him to speak. He appeared to contemplate a pattern of bullet holes that spelled out the letters V and R in the plaster of the wall, then turned back to the solemn group.

"Gentlemen," Holmes said, wiping tears of amusement away with the sleeve of his dressing gown. "Gentlemen, a good detective first uses observation, and second, reasoning and deduction."

"But we thought you wanted us to solve the case," Peachy protested.

Holmes held up a long slender finger to demand silence and leaned forward in his armchair. "A good detective only lastly . . . I repeat, gentlemen, lastly . . . acts on his conclusions. Not until all the brain work is done does he act, and then with caution and great care." Holmes looked each boy in the eyes, beginning with Peachy.

Peachy bit his lip and nodded his understanding.

"Gentlemen," Holmes said loudly, "I need you to be my eyes and ears, but that is all! Now go out and keep watch. And this time, if you see anything out of the ordinary, come tell me first before you do *anything* else. Do I make myself clear?"

"Yes, sir," Danny answered.

"We'll do it, just as you say, sir," Peachy agreed.

"Is that clear to you, Mr. Bernard?" Holmes asked Duff.

Duff smiled his understanding, then repeated, "Eyes and ears. That is all."

"Good," Sherlock Holmes concluded. "Now I have lots of work to do, so you boys go to it. Mrs. Hudson will show you out." Holmes stood and shook hands with each of them. "Don't be discouraged. You are bright and trainable, and I have confidence in you. Good day to you."

"Thank you, sir. We won't let you down," Danny said solemnly.

Relieved at being let off so easily and pleased to still be employed, the newly commissioned Baker Street Brigade turned and made their way down the stairs and out onto the street.

●●●

It was cold in the boys' dormitory of the Ragged School. The canvas curtains pulled over the boarded windows could not keep the cold, damp air from the river Thames from seeping into the drafty brick building. Seventy-nine boys from the ages of six to fourteen shared the sleeping quarters along with Danny, Peachy, and Duff. The gas lamps were turned down, and prayers had been said two hours ago.

Every boy was supposed to be sleeping, but Danny could not. Somebody on the other side of the blanket partition was crying softly. It made him sad, too, although he did not know why. He was too old to admit that sometimes in the night he wondered about his mother and his father and felt lonely. He was too old to cry, so he just listened to the younger child who was sobbing. It was as if the tears were for everyone in the room—for every boy without a mom or dad.

Danny snuggled deeper beneath the rough wool cover on his cot and squeezed his eyes shut. It had been a long day, and he was tired. But his mind drifted off to the headline about the kidnappings. Children stolen from their parents! It was a terrible thing, but Danny thought that it was not as terrible as the night his mother had left him on the steps of St. Paul's Cathedral and run away forever. He had been very small then, but he could still remember the sight of her back as she rounded the corner and vanished from his sight.

A gentleman had found him and brought him to the kindly Mr. Ingram here at the Ragged School. Danny had lived in this place ever since. He had cried a lot when he was very small, but he would not cry again.

In the next bed, Peachy groaned and turned over.

"Are you asleep, Peachy?" Danny whispered, hoping his friend was awake.

"What's that?" Peachy asked.

"It's Billy Little," Danny replied. "He's crying again."

"What's it about?" Peachy propped himself up on one elbow and peered through the darkness at the curtain that separated the big boys from the little ones.

Duff coughed and sniffed and said in a very sad voice, "It's about his muhver."

"His mother," Peachy corrected.

"That's what I said." Duff sat up in his bed. He made a big shadow on the brick wall. "I said his muhver."

"He'll get used to being here." Danny punched his pillow. "Then he'll quit crying at night."

"Maybe it's about his fahver," Duff went on.

"Father," Peachy corrected his big friend once more.

"Uh-huh," Duff agreed. "Billy wants to see his fahver."

"Duff! It's *father*. Ah, well, never mind! I just want him to forget about it and go to sleep." Peachy sounded angry.

Duff continued, "We all want Muhver and Fahver. Don't matter if we don't cry no more. We all want."

He was right. There were boys in the Ragged School who pretended they did not care, but everyone knew the truth. Each child was lonely after the lamps were turned down and just before sleep closed in. There was not one boy in the school who would not have done anything to have a real father and a real family.

"Well, wishing for a father won't make it happen," Peachy snapped.

"Nothing will make it happen," Danny agreed. He covered his head with his pillow, but he could still hear the sound of Billy's crying.

Duff coughed again. "I got a fahver."

From the darkness someone said loudly, "You was left at the back door of Black Friars Pub when you was a baby. All of us was left someplace. Or parents died. You ain't no different than the rest of us! You got no father, Duff Bernard!"

"I do," Duff insisted.

"Well," the voice challenged, "why ain't you with him then?"

Duff swung his legs over the side of the cot and stood up. His words were very loud. "Miss Chelsea—"

A loud mocking laugh rose from the far corners of the dormitory. "Did you hear that? Duff says Miss Chelsea is his dad!"

"No!" Duff shouted angrily. By now Billy's crying had stopped, and every boy in the room was awake. "Miss Chelsea says . . . I got a dad! She tells me he is right here with me all the time."

"I can't see him!" someone howled.

"Right here!" Duff thumped his chest.

"What's his name?"

Danny jumped out of bed and shouted for everyone to shut up. He put his arm around Duff's shoulders. "Come on, Duff. You're dreaming, mate."

Duff shook his head. "God," he said quietly and tapped his chest again, just above his heart. "Dad. Loves me . . . sees us here . . . you my brothers. Dad . . . Miss Chelsea says . . . he loves us and never will leave us no more." He turned toward the curtain and cupped his hands to call to Billy Little. "Don't you cry no more, Billy! Dad'll hold your heart while you sleep. Don't be lonely no more, Billy! He sees you! Even in the dark night. He sees everything!"

Now there was silence in the dormitory. So that was what Duff meant. He had a Father. Each of them had a Father. Life was not easy and the nights were long sometimes, but they were family.

And they were loved by Someone who would never abandon them or run away.

Four

In the heart of London, Trafalgar Square's centerpiece was the huge Nelson's Column, erected in honor of the great naval hero Lord Nelson. Nelson had led the British fleet to victory over the combined navies of France and Spain, but he had been killed in the battle on October 21, 1805.

The pillar stood 185 feet high with a 17-foot statue of Nelson at its top and towered over all other buildings or statues around. On this particular afternoon, the thin sunlight cast a long, hazy shadow, as if the square were a giant sundial. Colossal bronze lions guarded the base of the monolith. Nearby, two fountains gushed plumes of water that turned to white spray in the wind.

In between the two fountains stood another more modest statue—this one of General Charles "Chinese" Gordon, who had been killed in the Sudan only two years before. The life-size bronze had only recently been installed to the memory of the martyr of Khartoum.

"Ahhh, Gordon," newspaper foreman Mewsley said to the statue in between puffs of his foul-smelling cigar, "if only I'd have been there, that Mahdi scoundrel wouldn't have gotten away with it."

"Hello, Cap'n Mewsley," Danny said as he and Peachy and Duff arrived for their load of newspapers. The three were so used to Mewsley's odd habits that they took no notice of his conversation with the statue.

The headlines on the *Daily Telegraph* were mixed, one deploring the fourth kidnapping in less than two weeks, and the other stating that the Muslim rulers of the Sudan, known as the Mahdists, had proclaimed a state of holy war against all "infidels."

The second headline explained Mewsley's present babble. "But they wouldn't let me come. Wouldn't let none of us come to your aid! Ahhh, Gordon . . ."

"I say, good afternoon, Cap'n Mewsley," Danny repeated patiently, at last breaking through the man's reverie.

"Good day to you, lads. I was just apologizin' to General Gordon here for all the pigeons. They have already made quite a mess of him." He looked up at the figure again and took a long drag from his cheroot, accidentally blowing smoke in Danny's face.

Danny choked and coughed, but Mewsley didn't seem to notice.

"But I heard you talk about somebody gettin' killed," Duff said anxiously. "Was it pigeons that done it?"

Peachy elbowed him, but Duff paid no mind.

"Pigeons? No, no, Duff. Devils, let me tell you!" Mewsley exclaimed.

The four walked over to one of the fountains and sat down on the edge. Duff nestled close, excited that another story was about to be told.

"There was a man of the desert, called hisself the Mahdi. Said it was his right to take over all the land along the Nile. Wild men—dervishes, they was called—joined him. So, too, did the worst sort of cutthroats, slavers, and the like. He killed all who did not join him."

Duff's eyes widened, and even Peachy and Danny were fascinated by the story.

"So we sent our most famous general, Gordon, there." Mewsley poked at the statue with a crooked yellow-stained thumb. "Gordon was a strong man and a harsh one. He rounded up many of the bad 'uns. Even caught and executed the worst . . . had 'em shot, he did. Finally, the gen'ral, he went toe-to-toe, so to speak, with the Mahdi, but the Mahdi would not blink. That rotter give Gordon a deadline to cut and run or be killed."

"But Gordon didn't run, did he?" Duff asked, already knowing the answer.

"No, he didn't! Fact is, Gordon sent all the civvies—that's the ladies and the sprats, Duff—down the river in a boat and holed his-self up in the last great city left, Khartoum of bloody report."

Here Mewsley shook his fist at the sun as if rebuking the Mahdi to his face. So fierce was Mewsley's look that Duff peered upward to see where in the sky the villain was hiding.

Mewsley continued, "The gen'ral dug a great trench round the city, filled it with water, and gathered supplies, and then he dared that son of the sand to do his worst. See, he knew that we was just downriver with enough force to put paid to the Mahdi once and for all. Soon as the boat got through with Gordon's message, we would come on the double-quick."

Duff smiled, knowing the story would have a happy ending.

"But the message never came," Mewsley said.

Duff scowled.

"That boat with the women never made it to safety, and all the people in it died. So the British army never knew, and Gordon waited and waited. And some in the town were afraid of the Mahdi and run off in the night. Shame to their memory!"

"Was he all alone?" Peachy asked. "Did anybody stay at all?"

"Yes, a few of his loyal followers stayed, but very few. At the last, the water in his ditch fell, and the day came when the Mahdi launched his attack. Them dervishes, with their horrid yells and great long-barreled rifles, swept across the desert like a sandstorm and struck! General Gordon, who had loved and trusted many of those same people, was then killed at their hands."

"Oh, what a horrible end!" Danny said. "All alone. What a horrible end!"

Mewsley nodded. "Yes, a horrible end indeed, but by good fortune, that cursed Mahdi didn't live long enough to gloat! No, he died soon after. And it is said his followers blame Gordon and the rest of us Britishers for witchcraft or some such palaver. That's why the new Mahdi has declared this holy war against all us British infidels. The new man is usin' the idea of revenge to whip up his troops, don't you see?"

There was a pause before anyone spoke. Only the constant hiss of the fountains was heard. "Blimey," Danny said at last. "What an amazing man—that he would give his life for a whole country of foreigners just so they could have peace in their country."

"But, Cap'n Mewsley, how do you know so much about it?" Duff asked, puzzled.

"Well, Duffer, I was one of them soldiers waiting downriver. I would have give anything to fight and die alongside him."

After Mewsley finished the tale, the boys stood in silence for a while, looking up at the statue of a brave and proud man who gave his all for a people and a country so far away from his own.

•••

The boys had just sat down to their evening meal when Headmaster Ingram walked to their table to whisper to Danny, "You've a very important visitor."

Danny knew at once that it was Sherlock Holmes again. He quietly passed the news to Peachy, who puffed up with pride.

"Well," Peachy said loudly enough for his fellow students to hear, "a detective's work is never done."

The great thick wooden doors to the dining hall burst open, and Holmes stood in the doorway with Toby at his side. The keen-eyed detective looked right at the boys with a stern expression.

Had Mr. Holmes somehow heard Peachy's bragging?

Danny pulled Duff away from his third helping of codfish chowder by pointing toward Toby. The three friends left the hall, accompanied by humming conversation that Danny knew was all about them.

"We've work to do," Holmes said when he had them alone, "and it's serious. So you ought not go boasting to friends about it. They may end up less your friends than you think, for the right price. And if criminals get hold of them because of your wagging tongues, you would have endangered them, yourselves, and those we are trying to assist."

Peachy hung his head in guilty silence.

Danny swallowed hard, realizing the true danger they were facing.

"You are only just learning about this work, but knowing how to keep quiet is critical," Holmes scolded. "Now, tonight's work has required me to borrow Toby again, so as you might have deduced, we are to use him for his nose. We have a piece of the last child's clothing, and we know where the kidnappers were last spotted."

As he talked, Holmes led the group out of the school and down Pinchin Lane. "We are going at night because there will be less activity to distract our canine colleague. If Toby discovers anything this evening, that's where you boys will come in. Tomorrow you'll have to snoop around."

At York Road, Holmes hailed a carriage. While the boys struggled to load the fat dog, Holmes gave directions to the river. "Take us to Bishopsgate. I shall direct you from there." The carriage lurched forward. The scenery turned from shabby brick houses into larger buildings, some of which took up whole blocks and were multiple stories high.

Danny noticed some of the names like Touvell Traders and London Ltd. Shipping Insurance. Then the carriage turned north and crossed Blackfriars Bridge. Danny had a brief glimpse of the river, reflecting the thin crescent of an early evening moon, before it was hidden again by the stone-and-brick canyons of the business district.

Once over the bridge, they turned east on Queen Victoria Street past the poultry market, the fish market, and others. Danny watched

Toby sit up and sniff as they passed the buildings. The boy guessed that the dog was identifying each aroma in turn, perhaps testing himself in the gathering darkness. Danny closed his eyes and did the same, finding that he could indeed recognize a warehouse dealing in oranges and lemons and another that imported spices. When Danny opened his eyes again, he found that Toby had given up the game and was asleep on the floor of the carriage.

The ride seemed to be lasting forever until the pair of chestnut horses trotted past the Bank of England. Holmes rapped on the roof of the coach with the brass knob of his heavy cane, and the driver pulled the team to a halt.

Getting out of the carriage, Holmes paid the driver. "I have decided that we shall walk from here."

Danny climbed down, followed by Duff. Peachy and Danny tried to extract the sleeping dog. No matter how they coaxed, Toby opened only one eye, then rolled over with a groan.

"Toby, come!" Holmes called sharply.

But it was not until Duff repeated the detective's words that the mutt leaped from the carriage to his side.

"Well, Duff," Holmes remarked, "I see that you are exactly the right man for this job."

Danny and Peachy were amazed at Duff's control over the dog, but Sherlock Holmes got immediately down to business. He snapped a short leather leash onto the dog's collar and handed the lead to Danny. "Now, let me tell you why we did not take the carriage all the way to our actual destination," Holmes explained as the carriage rolled away. "I am continually being watched and followed by a number of my enemies, and I know for a fact that the coach was planted for our choosing. For though I did not recognize the driver, the carriage is definitely the same one that often waits for me outside my home in Baker Street."

"What've we gotten into, sir?" Peachy exclaimed.

"A commitment," Danny said under his breath. "We're stuck."

The group walked through an alleyway and emerged on Threadneedle Street. "Here we are," Holmes declared. The quartet and the dog stood in front of a large stately building with tall windows and a deep well all the way around, intended to provide light for windows on the walls below. The doorway was covered with an overhanging roof, supported by tall, thick columns. Danny read the brass plate at the door. GUILFORDS was all it said.

Holmes withdrew a folded piece of thick gray-and-red-striped wool from his pocket. "It was here that the kidnappers were seen emerging from their carriage with the child and changing to an unmarked delivery van before resuming their journey. But we might still have a chance of Toby following the scent. He has an amazing nose. This is a scarf that the child was wearing the same night he was abducted. It was found in the garden. If I'm correct, it should be enough to start Toby on the trail."

The sleuth knelt down next to the dog and let Toby sniff the cloth. As if recognizing that his time to perform had arrived, the dog stiffened his tail, and he furrowed the folds of skin over his eyes in concentration.

"Find, Toby, find," Holmes whispered over and over. Then, standing, he calmly said, "Go."

Toby looked once at Duff and bellowed a short, sharp howl. The dog bolted toward the end of the street, dragging a stumbling Danny, who was taken by surprise by the unexpected speed.

When the road angled to the left, Holmes called, "Stop." Toby stopped in a rigid pointed pose, with a smooth line running from nose to tail and his front left leg raised. Of course, the dog's rumpled fur and drooping ear spoiled the effect. It was an odd stance for such an ungainly animal. The picture made Danny think of someone like Mr. Sherman, the strange little taxidermist, putting on the red uniform of a guardsman and standing at attention.

When the rest of the group caught up, Holmes merely spoke the word "Go," and Toby was off again. This time Danny was prepared, and he jogged alongside Toby as the hound alternately sniffed the pavement and then raised his snout to snort a lungful of air.

And so it continued. The dog led them up and down streets so close together that Danny thought it was a mistake, They crossed

Threadneedle Street five times, three times from the north and twice from the other direction.

When Toby indicated that the trail was about to turn north again, the pursuit stopped to catch its breath, and Holmes explained. He reported that the kidnappers moved in that way on purpose to confuse the trackers, but even in a carriage, it was not working. Toby kept right on the scent, and at the next corner he turned east and pulled strongly straight ahead.

On Shoreditch High Street, the procession continued making its way past many ancient shops closed for the night and a few amused pedestrians.

Once they trotted past a blue-uniformed member of the Metropolitan Police. He tried to question Danny, but the dog's pace carried the boy past before the words came out. As Danny and then Peachy and then Duff ran by, each received a couple words of interrogation. "Here now . . . what's this . . . all about then?"

Holmes, bringing up the rear, answered for them all. "It's all right, Officer. They are with me."

"Oh, it's you, is it, Mr. Holmes? Well, all right then. I . . ." At that point the entire cavalcade rounded another corner, and the bobby was left to push up his domed helmet and scratch his puzzled head.

Every few minutes Holmes would call for Danny and Toby to wait until the group could catch up. On the last of these occasions he muttered, "I might be wrong for once. We're heading directly away from the river."

He ordered Danny to release the dog, and Toby ran a short distance into a dark alley and stopped. The hound barked frantically and pawed at a dark heap of something piled behind some abandoned crates.

From a distance the group thought it was the body of a child. A thrill of fear shot through Danny. What if the kidnappers had done something terrible? As Toby yelped and whined, the group burst into a sprint.

Finally they reached the dog and found him scratching at . . . a discarded pile of clothes.

"The scoundrels!" Holmes exclaimed. "They've stripped the child and dumped his things precisely to elude pursuit. They're more clever than I first suspected. Come, lads! Quickly now! There is a chance that Toby can still point the way, but we must help him. Wiggins, you follow the dog down this alley. The rest of us must spread out and comb the area. They may have tossed out a sock or cap somewhere else. We'll meet back here in ten minutes."

●●●

Peachy threaded among the pallets and crates, cautiously tiptoeing his way up the alley. He was half hoping that he would not be the lucky one to catch the criminals. After all, he thought, what would keep them from nabbing him just like the others? Alone in the darkness and the rising swirl of fog from the river, he could easily forget that he was following a trail already days old and that the kidnappers were unlikely to be anywhere close. His eyes were opened so wide that they hurt in a useless effort to see farther down the unlit alley.

The large buildings on either side that formed the narrow passage loomed up into the dark sky above. Their tops were masked by the thick blackness that seemed to increase with every step. The brick walls lost their color in the gloom, except for patches that caught the flickering reflection of the gas lamps out on the street. These bits of tint gave no comfort, though. They were shaded an eerie bloodred.

Peachy heard voices and froze where he stood, craning his head to listen. Any thought that he was supposed to be looking for clues flew out of his head. Then the stillness returned, and the only sound he heard was a ringing in his ears as if he was straining to hear as well as straining to see. The buzz was soon replaced by another sound—the hammering of his heart, pounding in his chest and then in his ears, rhythmically drowning out the ringing.

"Your heart's beating so loud, they'll find you first if you don't calm—," he said aloud to himself.

At that moment something grabbed him by the shoulder and

spun him around. He screamed, but it was cut off by a blow to his mouth that clasped over it.

"Here now. What are ye lurkin' about here for? Hold still and let me catch a squint of your face." The hands roughly jerked Peachy's face around toward the reflected lamplight. "Well, ain't this blue sky after the monsoon?" a burly figure said, laughing. "That ye and I should meet up again so soon. It's a rum 'un, it is. What're the chances?"

Peachy focused his eyes on the dense black beard and immense girth of his attacker. Oh no! It was the same man he had run from at the hulk with the dog.

"What've ye got to say for yourself, ye little spawn, before I scupper ye once and for all?"

"Please, sir," Peachy said when the grip over his mouth slacked off. "I'd forgotten all about you and the . . . uh, cat. Right? No, it was a . . . a mouse, wasn't it? See, I can't even remember."

"Stow that gammon. Ye expect me to believe that ye haven't told the authorities about my dognapping?"

"Why, yes, sir. I mean, no, sir. What I mean to say is . . . yes, I expect you to believe that I didn't put the crushers onto you. And I won't, neither."

"And why should I believe ye? Give me one good reason why I shouldn't burk ye right here, or wring your squealin' little neck."

"No!" Peachy shouted. "Look, when I found you that day I wasn't even looking for stolen dogs. It's none of my business. It's just that the dog in the rug seemed to be what I was looking for."

"Which was?" the sailor asked impatiently. "Speak up lad, and sheet it home sudden."

"Stolen children, mister. I was—and still am—looking for those kids who got kidnapped. You remember, from the papers?" Before the man could answer, Peachy continued, hoping that he could talk his way out of a broken neck. "Poor young children, taken from their parents at ages when they can't fend for themselves and don't understand what's happening to them. I'm an orphan myself, but not because I was stolen. Actually I don't know what happened to my parents, but I do know this. I can't sit around and let these thugs treat kids this way. I won't stand by and watch while happy families are torn apart by some menace out for a little spare change."

Peachy impressed himself with his glib speech. Now if it would only work on the ogre who still held him by the collar. "And I won't let happen to any more innocent children what I've mourned all my life," Peachy continued. "So you see, sir, when I saw the figure in the carpet struggling around, I thought . . . well, you know what I thought, so . . ."

"Blow me down! I'm sorry, lad. I'd no idea. It puts the wind in another quarter, don't it? Ye know, your tale reminds me of me. I been an orphink since I was three. Run off to sea when I was twelve. Many's the time I cried . . ."

Peachy looked up into the man's face and was startled to find the glint of a tear in the tough seaman's eye. "Look," Peachy interrupted, "I'm sorry, but I have to keep looking, or those kids may never be reunited with their folks."

"Right ye are, lad. Fair wind to ye then. And should ye need a dab hand in a fight—" the bearded figure thumped his chest—"Jack Whaley is your man." With that, the former sailor turned dognapper tossed Peachy in the direction of the exit from the alley.

Peachy wasted no time in putting several blocks between them. He quickly made up his mind to say nothing about the encounter to any of the others. No need to suffer any more embarrassment from Mr. Holmes.

Five

The next afternoon, Danny, Peachy, and Duff ate their lunch at the Embankment, overlooking the dark water of the river Thames. Duff climbed onto the back of the big bronze lion that guarded the tall Egyptian obelisk known as Cleopatra's Needle. He munched his apple and stared up at the strange writing carved on the ancient monument.

"Look there, will you? Pictures of big birds standin' over little cats. Bet the cats are scared of such big birds," Duff said in a serious tone.

Danny laughed. "Righto, Duff. That's what it says all right. In old Egypt, birds ate cats for supper. Not the other way around."

Peachy stood and stared up at the writing on the stone. "Wonder what it really means."

Danny shrugged. "Guess you have to be Egyptian to read it."

"No. It's too old. Even they don't write that way anymore in Egypt. It's all different," Peachy said as if he knew all about it.

"Birds eat cats in Egypt?" Duff was amazed.

"No," Peachy explained. "The pictures in the stone are letters.

High-ro . . . something. I forget. They mean something. A bird might stand for a big wind or a king . . . something."

"But what?" Duff scratched his head under his cap.

Peachy turned and tossed his apple core into the water. "Strange sort of writing. Like a stone newspaper, it is."

"Cor!" Duff breathed out. "Hate to carry a stack of *them!*"

Peachy and Danny laughed at the practical nature of Duff's concern.

"I bet Mr. Holmes could read it." Duff leaned his head to the side as if the angle would make the ancient writing easier to understand.

"Yes," Danny agreed. "To Mr. Holmes, everything means something."

Peachy sniffed and sat down on the cold stone step beside the lion. "Well, nothing meant anything last night. We are a flat bust as far as the detective business goes. Two tries, and we come up empty both times. Every clue is as impossible to understand as those silly Egyptian birds and cats and carved fellows dressed in bedsheets."

"We're just missing it somehow." Danny sighed and rested his chin in his hand.

Duff patted the bronze lion on the head. "Mr. Holmes says we should use our brains. All our brains. Think hard."

Danny and Peachy exchanged looks. Peachy rolled his eyes at Duff. "Think hard, eh? About what?"

Duff continued. "It means something," he said with assurance, patting the marble surface and tracing the outline of a carved snake with his forefinger.

"What means something?" Peachy was puzzled.

"Everything means somethin'," Duff said happily. "Clair has a cat. I seen her cat on her windowsill. A big yellow cat. I bet no Egyptian bird would eat that cat. Very big cat."

Danny frowned and tossed a crumb of his bread to a fat gray pigeon strutting on the sidewalk. The boys had failed to find even one shred of evidence. The trail had been lost. Not even Toby could sniff his way to the stolen children. What was left to be done?

"I bet Clair's cat would like to eat that pigeon," Duff rattled on.

"I've got it!" Peachy cried.

"You got the pigeon?" Duff asked. "No, you don't have it. Hullo, pigeon. There it is, you see, eatin' Danny's bread."

"No, Duff!" Peachy leaped to his feet, and the pigeon fluttered away. "I mean, I have an idea! Let's go have a word with Clair! After all, her father is a member of Scotland Yard. A police detective! Maybe he knows something about the mystery. Perhaps Clair has overheard some news about this dreadful kidnapping business."

Duff wagged his head and kicked at the sides of the bronze lion as if it were a horse to ride in the park. "Dread-fol. Dread-fol business. Full of dread. Uh-huh. Nappin' kids and birds eatin' cats and such. Can Clair read Egyptian letters, you think?"

He was still babbling as Danny and Peachy took off down the street toward Clair's house.

•••

A fishmonger, walking behind his horse-drawn cart, neared the home of Chief Inspector Avery. He rang a high-pitched bell and called, "Fresh fish! Mackerel! Halibut! Jellied eel! Nice fresh cod! Carp from the Thames! Come get your fish!" The fish seller held aloft a silver-scaled mackerel, displaying it like a trophy to the empty street. "Would you look at this fish!"

"Ouch!" a voice cried from a thicket of willow branches and ivy outside the brick wall of the Avery backyard. The tree shook oddly.

The fishmonger stopped in midsentence. Surprised, he gazed at the talking willow. He could not have been more perplexed if the mackerel itself had spoken. The street vendor shook his head, then gave the horse a good pop with the reins and continued onward. . . .

•••

Inside the willow thicket, Danny and Duff struggled to hoist Peachy up. "Push harder, mates," he said. "I can't see over the fence."

Danny strained on his toes, with Peachy's muddy foot pressed high above his head. With a disgusted sputter he spit out the glob of dirt that fell in his mouth. "What can you see?"

"Hang on. I can't see nothing with you two moving around and yapping every second."

"Hurry!" Danny snapped.

Duff stared lazily out through the gaps between the branches, paying no attention to the bantering boys. Bright shafts of light beamed in, illuminating their undercover observation.

The persistent dinging of the fishmonger's bell sparked a light in Duff's eyes. He raised his head like a bloodhound downwind from his criminal, sniffing the air. His nostrils flared, and he jerked his nose to the sky and howled, "Fiiiiish!"

"Duff, shhh!" Danny and Peachy hushed simultaneously.

"You're gonna get us caught," Peachy warned.

Duff could hardly stand it. Just the smell of fish gave him chills, and his mouth began to water. "Danny, I want some fish!" he pleaded.

Danny frowned. "Not now, Duff!"

"But, Danny, I haven't had any for a long time," Duff whined.

Peachy slapped a hand on the wall and glared down at him. "You had kippers for breakfast! Pipe down and hold still!"

Tears began to well up in Duff's eyes. Squinting, he pouted and made monkey lips.

Peachy brushed the branches aside and pulled himself higher. Lying across the wall on his belly, he peered down into Clair's garden. "Blimey, Clair really has it made."

"What can you see?" Danny blinked again because of the falling dirt.

"There's a lot of grass and a dolly and a hobbyhorse." The longing to be part of a family with such a yard was in Peachy's voice.

"Brilliant," Danny said, "but is she back there?"

"I don't see her, but as long as her father doesn't catch us, we'll be all right."

As the fish cart passed the bushes, Duff grew restless. He shifted his feet. "Danny, can't I just go look at the fish?"

"No," Danny answered. "There'll be plenty of time for that later."

"Oy." The fishmonger stopped outside the jungle of trees. "Whatcha doin' in there?"

"We're looking for our friend," Danny answered.

The fishmonger cocked his head to the side and pondered. "Whatcha lookin' for 'im in there for?"

"Well, sir, she lives here," Danny replied.

"I ain't never talked so much to a bush, but did you say she? You mean the little girl?" the fishmonger questioned.

"That's right. Clair Avery."

"You'll be right pleased to know that I saw her and her nanny come outta that front gate about ten minutes ago when I passed the first time."

"Peachy, did you hear that?" Danny shook Peachy's leg. "She's not here."

The man scratched his forehead and pushed back his cap. "I was countin' on a sale, but they said for me to come back later, 'cause they was on their way to Leadenhall Market."

"Peachy," Danny said, "come down. We got to go to the market."

Peachy scooted back on the wall, sliding his belly on the cold stone cap. Duff licked his lips and let go with one hand, leaning away from the barrier for a glimpse of the fish.

"Duff, hold still!" Peachy said grumpily. "I'm gonna fall."

But Duff's mind was evidently elsewhere. "Did you say you had mackerel?"

"I sure do," the man said proudly. "I have fourteen kinds of fish today and two kids of eels."

"Could I look at them?" Duff said, raising his eyebrows in anticipation.

"Oy, mate. Come have a look," the man said.

Duff let go of Peachy's foot.

"Duff, no!" Danny cried out. Peachy began to slide. His weight was too much for Danny. "Duff, come back!"

Danny crumpled to the ground. Peachy tumbled down on top of him and rolled into Duff's legs. The thicket shook and rattled.

In a moment of panic, Duff grasped the scrawny willow branch in front of him and slid downward. With a sound like cracking timber, the boy crashed onto the road with a *thud*.

The fishmonger's horse spooked, jerking loose the reins. The animal galloped off down the cobblestone street. Fins and scales went flopping in every direction, leaving a trail for the screaming vendor to follow.

Danny and Peachy scrambled to their feet. Outside the bushes, they saw the man running frantically down the lane. He shouted for his horse to stop, then stooped to pick up a cod and ran on in pursuit.

Duff lay there on the ground, still smiling, still thinking about fish.

The boys stood in shock for a minute, then started to laugh.

"Did you see that?" Peachy screeched.

"I don't think the fishmonger thinks it's funny," Danny pointed out.

The boys decided to join the search for the missing fish. They retrieved cod and mackerel, halibut and eels.

Duff picked up a particularly large flounder. "Can I keep it?" he asked hopefully as he returned it to the cart.

"No!" Danny said. "And that's the last. Come on now, double-quick, to Leadenhall Market."

The boys brushed themselves off and hurried away in the opposite direction of the muttering fishmonger.

Six

White-glass roofing suspended by a pale green wrought-iron framework sheltered the sawdust-covered floor of Leadenhall Market. Dozens of wooden stalls, piled high with meat and vegetables, as well as fruit and nuts from around the world, catered to every taste in London.

Danny strolled the covered path, scanning the booths from side to side, with one hand in his pocket. Peachy on his left and Duff behind were also searching for Clair, but she was nowhere in sight. On their right, a shopkeeper wielding a brass scoop trickled coffee beans into a chattering dish. The beam of the scale touched neither top nor bottom, but hovered precisely in the middle. The shopkeeper smiled at his customer, then plunged the scoop back into the barrel.

The smell of fresh plums aroused Peachy's appetite. Deep green Jerusalem avocados ripened in the warmth. Steam from the mass of shoppers condensed on the glass roof, then dripped, raining inside.

Danny cleared his throat. "No sign of Clair."

"Are you sure he said Leadenhall Market?" Peachy asked Duff, raising an eyebrow.

Duff tilted his head and scratched it thoughtfully. "I think so."

"She's here." Danny sighed. "We just have to put on our detective caps and find her."

"Look, there she is!" Duff, able to see above the rest, pointed his long thick finger over some oranges, past a shopkeeper, and toward the crowd on the other side.

"Where?" Peachy said doubtfully.

"I see her," Danny said, reaching his arm over Peachy's shoulder. He gestured at a pastry stand three aisles over. "There she is, with her nanny, by that pillar."

"Right you are," Peachy remarked.

Clair wore a pink dress with a lace collar and a bow in the back. In her right hand she held a beaded blue handbag. Mrs. Fleming, the Averys' housekeeper, received a white paper sack and handed over some coins. Clair looked on, her index finger beside her mouth. Mrs. Fleming walked away, leaving Clair alone.

"Isn't she pretty?" Danny gawked.

"She sure is," Peachy agreed, "but that bloke behind her looks dodgy." He pointed to a dark shape lurking in the shadows behind Clair.

A sinister figure in a black cloak edged closer to Clair. Danny anxiously stepped toward the fruit stand. "You're right. He's stalking her! Clair!" he shouted in warning.

She turned at the sound of her name being called, but the mob of shoppers closed the gap just before she saw the boys. When the path cleared again, Danny saw the robed man lunge for the girl. A long black sleeve reached around Clair to cover her mouth.

"Clair!" Danny shouted again, leaping to help but falling chest first into the pile of oranges.

Clair's eyes filled with fright. The hooded scoundrel met Danny eye to eye, piercing the mist and distance with his glare.

Grasping his wiry forearms with her fragile hands, Clair kicked wildly. The muscles in her cheeks flexed, her jaw clenched. Clair's teeth bit hard into the man's palm.

Screaming and cursing in a foreign tongue, the villain yanked his hand back, freeing her. He made a grab for her purse, twisting it loose from her grip, and escaped to the back of the market, into the deep shadows of the building behind.

Danny pushed himself off the merchant's table. Scads of oranges avalanched to the ground. They bounced off his feet and rolled under tables as he leaped in pursuit.

Peachy followed. "Duff, stay with her!"

Charging up the aisle with his elbows out and head down, Danny burst through the crowd like a locomotive. Knocking down a cook, a parson, two housewives, and an organ-grinder, he slid around a candy counter. The sawdust greased the soles of his worn black boots. He slipped again, barely missing a butcher's cart that entered the courtyard in front of him.

Peachy, right on Danny's heels, crashed into the cart, flipping it over on top of him. Pork sausages and smoked hams went flying through the air to land under a stairwell. Twenty-two alley cats were treated to an unexpected feast.

Danny continued alone down a passageway, through a corridor, and into the street. A police whistle sounded somewhere behind him, muffled by the chaotic noises of the courtyard.

Danny spotted the thief crossing an intersection down the road, then veering into a side street. Danny's pursuit plunged him in front of a team of horses. The driver of the carriage fought the reins. The horses reared and kicked, narrowly missing Danny's head.

Tracing the man's flight, the boy ran up the street, turning right down the brick lane. He could hear his own and the thief's feet punching the ground in a fast rhythm, like a sewing machine.

The thief skidded around a smoke-stained corner, his robes trailing behind. Danny ventured after, finding himself in a narrow dead-end alley.

The panting thief grabbed the tall drainpipe on the wall, stuck his sandaled feet in the narrow cracks of the chipped bricks, and began to climb. He was several feet above the ground when Danny reached him.

Danny vaulted upward. His fingers seized the tattered hem of the dark cloak.

The man struggled. Try as he might, he could not overcome the drag of Danny's weight pulling him backward. The attacker's grip began to slide downward on the pipe, his hands squeaking on the painted metal of the drain. He unleashed a flurry of kicks, first to Danny's arm, then a hard blow to Danny's forehead.

Danny hung with both feet off the pavement, hoping that Peachy would arrive in time to help.

The weakening fibers of the robe loosened. A *rip* sounded as the cloth stretched.

The man shouted, then kicked again. Danny's grasp, tight on the hem of the cloak, held firm, but a piece of fabric tore free. Danny tumbled back, swinging his arms for balance, as Clair's assailant landed another solid blow to the top of the boy's head.

Danny fell hard. Crashing onto his hip drove the wind out of him with a cry of pain. His neck snapped back, cracking his head on the bricks.

Danny watched with hazy vision as the would-be kidnapper scurried up the pipe and escaped over the top of the building.

In his mouth there was a metallic taste. It overwhelmed all of his other senses.

Relaxing his grip on the cloth, he closed his eyes.

•••

Danny awoke to a slight drizzle of water on his forehead. He made a feeble gesture with one hand to wipe off the moisture and vaguely wondered why he was lying out in the rain. A second sweeping motion of his hand encountered a muscular arm, and Danny's eyes snapped open.

Duff was kneeling beside him in the alleyway with a pitcher of water, gently pouring it over his head. It pooled in the folds of a cloak that Mrs. Fleming, Clair's nanny, had placed under him like a pillow.

"You fell bad," Duff said with concern.

Danny saw a ring of concerned onlookers standing around him. He saw Clair, Peachy, Mrs. Fleming, and a new face that seemed to have a dome-shaped top. Danny's head throbbed, and his eyes refused to focus on the upside-down image. He could not figure out who the unknown onlooker was until he noticed the dark blue uniform of a bobby. The unusual shape of the man's head resolved into a helmet.

The policeman walked around to Danny's feet and stood gazing down at the boy. "Foolish, lad. Brave, but very foolish. You're lucky you've woken up at all from a knock like that."

Danny stared back, only able to make out the man's handlebar mustache amid the halo of unnaturally bright sunlight behind him. "But I had to," Danny said. "He was going to kidnap Clair."

"No, lad, you are mistaken. It was merely a petty theft. He didn't even get away with anything valuable. After all," the policeman scoffed, "nothing of value would ever be in a little girl's purse."

Clair became indignant at the remark. "Well, I think it was very brave, and you are not one to talk. After all," she chided, "you did nothing at all!"

"Clair," her nanny scolded, "that's no way for a young lady to speak to a constable!" Mrs. Fleming thanked the officer.

The man excused himself, saying he had to go make his report about the incident, which he now considered closed. "If you and the young miss will accompany me, please, mum. The young chap there will be all right. Tough as shoe leather, he is. Be right as rain in no time."

Clair started to protest that she did not want to leave until Danny was up and around, but Mrs. Fleming insisted that for Clair to remain in the alley was not proper. The girl was forced to leave them, but not before she gave Danny a grateful look.

"Maybe the peeler's right, Danny," Peachy said after the trio had departed. "He did steal her purse."

"But you saw it for yourself. That bloke, whoever he was, was grabbing for Clair, not her purse. He didn't even make a move to take it until he saw us coming toward him." Danny tried to sit up, but an explosion as bright as the photographer's flash powder went off inside his head, and he groaned and lay down again.

Duff continued to splash water on Danny's face, but the water had become an annoying drip that tapped Danny's forehead as he talked with Peachy. "Duff, I'm fine now. You can stop with the water," Danny suggested.

Duff backed away as Danny sat up again, this time with success. He gingerly felt the back of his skull and was amazed to find a lump the size of a grapefruit. "Come on. Let's go talk to Mr. Holmes. He'll know what's going on."

•••

The Baker Street Brigade burst through the outside door of 221B Baker Street and tromped loudly up to the second-story sitting room. Peachy pounded on Mr. Holmes's door. There was a long pause, interspersed with the rattle of glassware and an unknown low hissing noise.

"Blimey," Peachy muttered. "Think he's charming a snake in there? And what's that smell?"

"His eggs has gone bad," Duff suggested.

"Come in, wharf rats," Holmes invited.

Danny turned the squeaky knob, swinging the door wide. In an instant, a huge yellowish mist rolled toward them, a sinister poisonous fog with the unbearable stench of sulfur.

Danny entered cautiously, coughing into his fist, with Duff behind him. Peachy shut the door, causing a puff of amber vapor to be trapped in the hallway . . . like a little lost cloud.

In the corner of the room, between the fireplace and the window, stood Sherlock Holmes. His back was to them. In front of him, on a table, stood dozens of cylindrical glass tubes filled with solutions of many colors. The hissing noise came from a small gas burner that flared beneath a potbellied flask.

Danny thought Peachy had been right about the snake. Then he saw that the brown coils draped from the lamp on the wall to the table were nothing more than a rubber hose that fed the gas from the outlet to the burner.

In the glass container over the flames swirled a bubbling yellow liquid. The long tapering snout of the flask was connected with another glass tube from which an emerald green fluid spiraled downward. The whole apparatus popped and fizzed, opening a pressure release at the top. From it came the yellow steam that smelled so terribly like rotten eggs. The boys watched the scene with amazement.

Holmes's sleeves were rolled to his elbows. Long black rubber gloves stretched from his turned-back cuffs to his fingertips. A matching black rubber apron hung from his neck and was tied around his waist . He wore a pair of bulging lensed goggles that made him look remarkably fishlike. "Ha," Holmes exclaimed, turning to greet them. "What brings the day?"

All the boys began to speak at once.

"A man snatched our friend, Clair, then climbed a pipe," Danny began.

"She bit him and we chased him," Peachy continued.

"They ran after him, and the cats ate the ham," Duff added.

"One at a time!" Holmes commanded loudly. "You, Wiggins, report. You others must wait your turns."

The boys quieted, and Danny explained.

Holmes listened thoughtfully, contemplating every word. "So when you found Clair, Chief Inspector Avery's daughter, you thought she might have heard something useful. So far, very good. Then a man tried to kidnap her, you say, in the middle of Leadenhall Market at the busiest time of day?" Holmes raised his eyebrows and laced together his black-gloved fingers.

"Yes, sir," Danny anxiously replied. "But when I went to grab him, he kicked me. I fell and was knocked out."

Holmes gestured for Danny to come nearer. The detective reached for the boy's chin, gently turning it to examine the goose egg on the back of Danny's head. "And quite a hard knock, I see."

Danny smiled ruefully and rubbed the knot on his skull. "Yes, well, he got away with her purse, but I managed to get this." Danny held out the narrow piece of black fabric, which he had torn loose from the cloak.

Holmes snatched the cloth from him and held it up to the light. "It looks to be staple Egyptian cotton. The dye is Phoenician Black. Hold on a moment while I run a complete analysis on it."

Holmes returned to his chemistry table, pulling the burner away from under his experiment. He snipped two small pieces from the tattered material, charring one to ashes in the flame of the burner. The other he placed on his microscope for examination. Adjusting the mirror and then the piece of fabric, he pulled the object into focus. "Yes, it's definitely Egyptian, a poor weave, and the dye . . ." He paused to place the ashes in a shallow dish to which he added a drop of liquid from a clear bottle with a ground glass stopper. The black ashes bubbled, and a thin trail of smoke rose from the dish. "And the dye is . . . yes, Phoenician Black." The private investigator extinguished the flame of the burner by twisting a knob on its base, and the flame disappeared with a soft pop.

Holmes rejoined the group, stopping in front of Duff. "I am something of an expert at recognizing the origin of cloth from its ashes," he said. "I've written a monograph covering more than three hundred weaves of fabric."

Duff rubbed his chin and nodded wisely.

"So what do you think, Mr. Holmes, sir?" Peachy interrupted.

"It was probably a robbery," Holmes said simply.

Danny frowned. "A robbery, but he covered her mouth and tried to drag her out of sight."

Holmes smiled slightly. "To keep from attracting attention."

"But he tried to take her," Peachy insisted.

"No, it only looked like it. May I remind you of the last time you jumped to conclusions?" Holmes said arrogantly. "This was obviously a robbery. Nothing else makes sense. It cannot be anything connected with the string of kidnappings."

Danny stood up to him. "But you said never assume the obvious."

"That's right," Holmes snapped. "Unless it's obviously the truth!"

"But how do you know it's the truth?" Peachy asked.

"Simple," Holmes replied. "The fabric is Egyptian. What do any of the families have in connection with Egypt? Nothing. Moreover, it is a poor grade of cloth worn by half the foreigners in the East End, I daresay. Also, let me remind you that all of the kidnapped children are boys. Finally, no one in his right mind would try to take the chief inspector's daughter in broad daylight. No, gentlemen," Holmes concluded, "this is evidence of how rampant petty crime has become in London streets—nothing more."

"Um," Danny sighed with defeat.

Peachy stared at the floor, while Duff chewed on his lip.

"I guess you're right, sir," Peachy said, sounding disappointed.

"Of course I'm right," Holmes assured them. Then in a more kindly tone he said, "But I will credit you for being on the scene where *a* crime was committed. If you want to follow up on your lead . . ." He walked over to his desk and tore off a sheet from his personalized notepad. "Take this note to the taxidermist shop in Lambeth. Sherman will give you Toby, as well as instruct you in any commands he might need."

Duff's eyes lit up with excitement. "Toby!"

Danny and Peachy could hardly believe their ears. "It will be good practice for you, and who knows what might turn up," Holmes said, handing them the paper. "In any case, the kidnapping affair is about to break open, I believe. On the day after tomorrow, I'll be in disguise on the scene at the money drop for the third victim."

"Can we go?" Peachy asked.

"No, I'm afraid it must remain a very secret operation. But see what you can find and report back," Holmes emphasized. "We'll compare notes. So run along, and tomorrow, first thing, get Toby."

"Thanks, sir," Danny said gratefully.

Peachy waved. "We'll get the kidnappers yet—you'll see."

"Good-bye . . . and good luck." Holmes grinned, opening the door.

"Just one more thing," Danny asked, pausing at the exit. "What experiment were you working on when we arrived?"

"Right," Peachy agreed. "Someone been attacking swell gents with rotten eggs?"

"No, lads," Holmes chuckled. "I wish it were that simple. What you smelled was sulfuric acid reacting with another substance. I'm working on a case involving a deadly new type of explosive. Perhaps I can tell you more about it later."

The eyes of Peachy and Danny grew wide with excitement. Explosives! And Mr. Holmes might want their assistance!

Duff, the last one through the door, nodded to the detective on his way out. "Cor! We get Toby!" he said, and the door shut behind him.

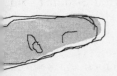

Seven

Past the awful-smelling tanning yard on the left and the butcher's shop on the right, Danny and Duff advanced down Pinchin Lane. "That tannery smells like Mr. Holmes's experiment," Danny remarked.

Danny rapped gingerly with his skinned, bruised knuckles on the entry of the taxidermy shop. The knocking, soft as it was, set off an uproar of mixed barks, howls, screeches, and other less easily identified sounds. The thin pane of glass in the shopwindow rattled loudly.

The owner, Mr. Sherman, sprang to the second-story window above them and shouted, "Go away before I sic the dogs on you! Go away, I say!" His scraggly fringe of hair was matted on one side of his spotted head and stood straight up in wiry tufts on the other. "Go away, I tell you. I don't collect kids, except to feed them to the lions." Ill-fitting false teeth made him spray spit as he talked.

Duff looked frightened by the gruff old man, as if he were ready to run. But Danny merely squinted upward and stepped aside to avoid the spit. "Sir, we've come for Toby."

"Toby doesn't live here!" Sherman screamed, slamming the window.

Duff pulled his neck and chin back like a bullfrog. He looked as ready to leap as a frog.

Danny huffed, "Crazy mountain goat. Just you hang on, Duff. I'll see this put right, I will. Dotty old fool."

The window went flying open again with a crash. "I heard that, you spindly little jackanapes. Get out of here before I sic my badger on you. He's vicious, you know . . . has the rabies. Don't believe what you read in the papers, neither. There ain't no cure for the rabies. Don't matter what that Frenchy Pasteur says."

"Ha!" Danny laughed loudly to show he was not afraid. "Right you are, I'm sure, Mr. Sherman, and Sherlock Holmes didn't send us, either."

"What? Who? Did you say Sherlock Holmes?" Sherman asked curiously.

"We're on a secret investigation for Mr. Holmes, and we need Toby," Danny said with authority. "Quickly, please. It's important."

"Well, why did you not say so?" The proprietor slammed the window again. Footsteps tromped loudly around the top floor for a moment. Then a bucket or some similar object was heard bounding down the interior stairs. The roars and squawks, which had subsided, rose again.

Duff turned to Danny. "I hope he doesn't kill us and stuff us like birds. I don't think I would look good standin' in his window." With a mournful look on his face, Duff gestured at the stuffed owl.

Danny shook his head. "Too right—you wouldn't, mate. But don't you worry. Just be on guard." A sly grin crept across his face as he spoke.

Frenzied barking grew louder as the man approached the door. "Be still, children. Hush then. Get by, Nipper. Be off with you!" It seemed that Mr. Sherman had to address each of his charges as he passed. "What do you want again?" Sherman yelled, opening the front door.

"Sir, we want to take Toby," Danny repeated, handing over the scrap of paper from the detective's pad. "Here's a note from Mr. Holmes."

Sherman snatched the message from Danny's hand. He read it silently, with his jaw clenched. Then he looked up, probing the boys' eyes, as if checking to see if they were telling the truth. He decided at last that they were. "No sense wasting my whole day! Come in! Lively now, lively!"

The taxidermist stood aside as Danny and Duff entered.

Inside, the building reeked of dung and the warm, sharp odors of hundreds of animals. The floor was covered with thick straw, and the walls were coated with cobwebs. Stepping over a dark green-and-brown python, the boys passed a small black bear chained to a post. "Stay away from him," Sherman warned them, jerking a crooked thumb at the bear. "He tore off a mule's leg only last week. Naughty! Naughty!"

Danny and Duff continued to follow, though Danny was unsure of what Holmes had gotten them into.

Danny felt Duff's big hand tugging at his shoulder.

"Danny!" Duff whispered hoarsely.

"What?" Danny replied.

"It stinks in here."

Sherman turned around in the dingy hallway, placing both hands on his hips. In a stall to his right were a horse, two pigs, and several geese. The taxidermist leaned close to Danny and Duff and, with foul breath, said, "Animals got rights—same as you, don't they?"

Duff took two steps back. His eyes were wide. "Yes, sir," he said quickly.

Sherman sniffed. "They don't care for the smell of you neither." Then he continued through the building that was really more barn than shop.

At the end of the hallway he stopped, reaching toward a nail on the wall. On it hung a leather leash. "Here," he said crisply, handing the strap to Danny. "Cheerio, Toby. Daddy's gonna let you out for a while." Sherman squatted down to speak into the dog cage. He reached in his shirt and juggled a set of keys. It was a heavy rusty set of twenty or more, Danny saw, and the locks on Toby's cage required the use of three of them.

The boys stood staring silently as Sherman fumbled around, trying to find the right keys. "Aha, someone's switched the order on me," the man announced, finally opening the last lock. "He's valuable property, you know. Can't be too careful."

Danny wondered what thief in his right mind would ever attempt to steal anything from this chamber of horrors. A large black hairy spider strolled lazily over Sherman's hand as it rested on top of Toby's crate. "Hello, Esmerelda. Come to see about the excitement?"

Toby, happy to see company, barked loudly, spinning around in circles. Duff let him lick his hand and face. "Him a happy dog."

"I think he's taken with you," Sherman said thoughtfully, studying the hound as if it could be ill. Then the man looked back at Duff and snapped, "But that don't mean you can keep him."

Danny reached down to pet the hound's wavy red-brown-white fur and to scratch him behind the ears. "We'll bring him back safe and sound, just as soon as we find the kidnappers."

"Kidnappers, eh?" Sherman glanced at Danny, with his hand on his scruffy chin. "Hmmm. Toby's your boy, right enough. There's only four things you need to know. *Go. Find. Stop.* And *Come.* You got those?" Sherman took the leash from Danny and hooked it onto Toby's collar.

Danny nodded. "Piece of cake. We were with Mr. Holmes and Toby the other night."

"Good," Sherman said, handing Duff the leash. "Then be off with you, before I throw you mice into the snake pit. The vipers are getting hungry."

Duff's eyes bulged. He covered his mouth with his hand and hurriedly followed Danny out, with Toby trailing obligingly behind.

●●●

Leadenhall Market was as lively as ever. Vendors, shoppers, and beggars filled the scene. Danny entered the passage along which he had chased Clair's attacker the day before. Duff gripped the leash tightly as Danny turned Toby onto the scent with the wadded fragment of cloth. "Find," Danny commanded.

The dog instantly found the scent and, with a howl, strained on the leash. Duff was pulled along on the trail of the purse thief.

Out to the cobblestone street they ran in a drizzling rain under hazy gray skies. Across the courtyard and up the brick lane Toby took them. He led the way down the lane and into the alley, right up to the drainpipe, until stopping at last exactly where Danny had fallen.

"Cor! He does know his business, then!" Danny observed. "Find," he ordered again.

Toby stood on two legs, stretching upward against the wall. "Find," Danny shouted. "You can't climb, you daft dog."

Duff looked at Danny with reproach. "He's doing his best."

Eager to please, the dog barked through the alley to the lane, then turned right, circling the building over which the thief had fled. Across the slick cobblestones he towed Duff, whose heavy feet slapped the ground like hooves of a heavily loaded pack animal.

Right again at the end of the lane, Toby led them along a sidewalk past the front of a block of newly built flats. The apartments were three stories tall and the structure a whole block in length. At the top of the road, Toby's nose hit the stone again. He sniffed wildly around a lamppost, then raised his head and let out a glorious yelp. He was back on the trail, and Duff with him.

"Duff, wait up!" Danny called, tired from the fast pace of their sleuthing expedition. The truth was, Danny's head ached miserably from being smashed into the paving stone. The pounding going on inside his skull felt louder than the sound of the bells of St. Katharine Cree, though the church was just a block away and right then ringing out eleven o'clock.

"I can't," Duff called back. "He really wants to go!"

Toby turned the next corner at full speed, cut down a side street into another alley, and stopped directly over a manhole cover. Duff wheezed to a halt, with his hands wrapped around his middle, as if trying to catch his breath.

Seconds later Danny also came to a stop next to Duff and the hound, who was barking and bouncing up and down on the metal lid.

"Oh no," Danny said with disappointment.

"Into the sewer," Duff repeated. "We'll never find him now."

Danny felt the lump on the back of his head and agreed that they had done enough for one day. His heart beat fast. "Never mind, Duff. We've got the dog and the scent. He's bound to turn up again."

"I not goin' in no sewer," Duff reasoned, shaking his head. "There's big rats in there."

"It's all right, Duff. I don't think Toby likes the sewer either. Do you, lad?"

Toby gazed up at him with sad eyes and whimpered. He knew he could do no more.

Danny bent down to pet him. "That's a good boy. You did a good job." Toby wagged his tail. "Come along then, Duff," Danny patted his big friend on the back. "No rats today. Let's give it up for now."

Duff smiled, and the three of them headed for home.

• • •

The sky over London was bleak, heavy with dark clouds that were ready to burst with rain. Trafalgar Square, though, was still busy. People hurried from office to shop, from making money to spending it. Pigeons wandered about, looking for crumbs or bits of discarded noon meals. The fountains provided a constant background, hissing all day behind various conversations, some relaxed and unimportant, some dangerous and secretive.

"Well, lads." Mewsley addressed his soldiers in the newspaper wars. "Another hard day's work done and gone, eh?"

"Yes, sir, Cap'n Mewsley," Peachy replied, "and we've nothing else to do for an hour or so."

"So tell us a story," Duff said. "One with a happy finish."

"Ahhh, you want the good 'uns to win for once, eh, Duffer? That I can do."

Danny saw a tattered beggar sitting nearby, but he paid him no heed. Beggars were always at Trafalgar Square, hoping for handouts from tourists.

•••

As the group of newsies sat down by the fountain, a one-legged beggar moved closer, very intent on listening in to the story about to be told. He had long dirty hair and tattered clothes with torn fringes. One eyelid sagged, and crooked teeth jutted randomly over his bottom lip.

•••

"It was a long time ago," Mewsley said, "back in Africa. We was holdin' garrison duty, keepin' the situation there under control."

"From what?" Danny asked.

"Why, from the Mahdists, of course. Well, one mornin' at parade, the sergeant major found that the count was one over. Now that was a right peculiar thing because usually the buckoes ran *away* from the army. Not the other way round." Mewsley laughed at his own joke.

He paused to fling away the half-inch-long stub of his cheroot and light another before continuing. "So Sergeant Major O'Meara recounted, findin' the same mismatch in number. Now O'Meara was a deft one, he was. He hollers to us, 'You men all look about at your neighbors, and if you glam anything what don't belong, give a shout to wake the dead!'" Mewsley imitated the Irish sergeant's accent, and the boys howled with laughter.

"So what happened?" Duff asked eagerly.

"Well, I turns this way," Mewsley said, slowly pivoting to the left and fixing a beady stare on Danny, "and I turns this way." He turned partway toward Duff, then paused, squinting up at Gordon's statue. The peculiar stare on Mewsley's face suggested that he had indeed noticed something a bit out of place. "Wait one minute, boys. I've got to investigate somethin'."

As Mewsley climbed up on the statue, Danny and Peachy

speculated about the outcome of the story. Their foreman reached up into the crook of the bronze left arm of Gordon's likeness and retrieved a small paper bundle tied with twine.

Stepping down from the pedestal with the package in hand, Mewsley intoned, "Hello, what have we . . . ?"

Then, suddenly, the nearby beggar rose upright . . . and became taller than he could possibly have been on one leg.

Duff yelped.

Danny and Peachy watched in horror as the ragged figure began peeling off parts of his face.

Just as Mewsley turned to inquire about the wail of alarm coming from Duff, the supposed beggar dug his fingers into the top of his forehead and shucked off his face to reveal a new one.

Sherlock Holmes tossed aside the filthy rags that covered his clean suit and dropped the rubber mask and scraggly wig on top of them. He withdrew from his pocket the shiny silver tube of a Metropolitan Police whistle and blew it loudly.

From across the street from the square, from the entrance to the crypt of the church of St. Martin-in-the-Fields, burst a horde of blue-coated policemen. At a second blast of the shrill summons, still more bobbies rushed toward Trafalgar from other buildings around the square. Inspector Avery, Clair's father, approached from inside the lobby of the church, with two burly uniformed men at his side.

"There he is, Inspector." Holmes pointed a long accusing finger at Mewsley. "That is your kidnapping culprit."

What? Danny couldn't have been more shocked. And from their faces, Mewsley, Duff, and Peachy were, too. Duff still whimpered from the fright of seeing a man take off his own face, while Danny and Peachy shouted questions excitedly at the great detective.

Mewsley stood calm and still as the policeman took the package, bound his wrists behind his back, and tied his ankles loosely together. Roughly pushed by one of the guards, he stumbled toward the grim, windowless police carriage known as Black Maria.

Before he was shoved into the coach, he said only one thing.

"Trust me, boys. I don't follow what this is about, but it was not me what done it."

"Boys, boys!" Holmes shouted to stop the avalanche of inquiries. "I can only answer one question at a time, but better that I tell you the whole story at once to save time."

Danny and Peachy fell silent. Duff scowled.

"Now, since the last kidnapping, I have been involved with Scotland Yard in a plan to arrest the kidnapper when he came for the ransom money, which your foreman Mewsley just did."

"But he's not a . . . ," Danny tried to explain.

"Criminal?" Holmes stated. "Ha! I've looked into the history of this man, and it appears that he is." He took a paper from his front waistcoat pocket and read aloud. "In '56, he was arrested for stealing while on active duty in Her Majesty's service. In '58, he was flogged for trafficking in stolen goods. In '72, he—"

"All right!" Danny yelled. "All right, maybe he was in trouble with the law before, but why now? He's good to us and a hard worker. How can you be sure he's guilty?"

"Elementary, my dear Wiggins. Consider his fingers."

Danny looked puzzled.

"The same dirty, yellow-stained fingers that the nanny who witnessed the Caravaldi kidnapping described are present on your foreman, caused by those foul-smelling cheroots." Holmes crossed his arms, looking satisfied.

Danny felt sick. The clue had been in the papers the whole time, and they never noticed. "I can't believe it. But we've been with him almost every day. Why didn't you tell us so we could watch him closer?"

"No, no, my lad," Holmes comforted him. "Had you three been anything but natural in your daily habits, our criminal would have smelled foul and fled. No, had you known, you could not have done better."

Danny supposed that it must be true, but somehow it didn't feel right.

And just then the clouds burst forth in a cold drenching rain.

Within minutes Trafalgar Square, emptied of people and pigeons, was deserted and forlorn.

•••

Mindless groans pierced the blackness. Like dangerous animals, men and women were chained to the cold stone floors of Newgate Prison. Jail fever and typhoid lurked around the corner from every cell. Sewer rats victimized the flesh of any unwary prisoners.

All the while, high above this sinkhole of imprisoned humans, the shadows of the free appeared on the cell walls. Skylights at ground level on the busy London street gave the prisoners constant reminders of how near—and unattainable—freedom was. It added to the torment.

The creak of a heavy steel door echoed down the corridors, followed by a slamming noise. Thick-soled boots splashed through puddles as the keeper drew near Mewsley's cell. The guard jingled his keys and whistled an off-key music-hall song.

Mewsley rushed to the bars that filled the tiny window in his cell door.

"Visitors, Mewsley," the warder said gruffly. "You've got two minutes." The man turned and walked up to the observation chamber at the top of the stairs.

"Cap'n! Cap'n!" cried Danny and Peachy, rushing to the bars.

"My boys," Mewsley said, reaching swollen arms through the bars to hug them.

"What have they done to you?" Danny cried, gripping his friend's hands and staring with horror at the blackened eyes and split lip.

"Beat me good, they did. Kept me up all night, grillin' me about some kidnappin'." Mewsley winced as some pain stuck him.

"But why, Cap'n? Why?" Peachy said, a tear welling up in his eye.

"They think I done it. Say I went straight to the money. They want to know who I'm workin' with. How can I tell 'em what I don't know?" Mewsley broke down and began to sob. "I never did nothin' to hurt nobody. They says I got the yellow fingers, and so I does, but I know they ain't been on no kid. Stealin' they says I was in the army, and sent down for it, but I'd never hurt no kids. You know that! I love all you sprats." He sniffed and wiped the tears from his eyes with his palm. "I gotta be strong. I gotta be strong now for you kids."

"We know you're innocent, Cap'n Mewsley," Danny said with certainty. "We got ourselves a good bloodhound named Toby. We'll catch the real kidnappers and prove you innocent."

"But they want to know who I'm workin' with." Mewsley began to cry again. "Don't you see? They beat me so I'll tell 'em. But I don't know nothin' except for the African wars, the Mahdi and the Sudan." He moaned softly.

"Cap'n," Danny said, "we've been talking to God about you. Master Ingram says you'll be all right, and he gave us a Scripture to give you." Danny reached in his pocket and pulled out a crumpled scrap of paper. "John 8:32 says, 'You shall know the truth, and the truth shall make you free.'"

Mewsley quieted down. "It's true. I ain't guilty, so it'll all get put right. It was nice of you boys to remember me down here. You and that Scripture put me in mind of how good I felt to see mornin' come after the battle at Rorke's Drift. And that was a tougher scrape than this, I will say."

Danny breathed a sigh of relief. If their friend could once again be reminded of his war stories, then he had not completely given up in despair.

But Peachy stared blankly at Mewsley's fingers and pondered the evidence of the yellow stains and the money. It was the first time he'd ever seen Mewsley without a cigar.

Eight

As was the habit at the Avery home, a saucer of milk was set outside the front door for any stray cats that may be in the neighborhood. It had been a task Clair's mother performed, but since she was gone, Clair was taking on more and more responsibility, trying to keep things the way they used to be.

The door creaked open, and the cold frost in the night air bit at her toes. She was wrapped in a dark green dressing gown that reached the stone steps below her as she leaned out and set the saucer down.

"Toodles," she called, "here's a late-night snack for you." Clair and her mother had named the strays, and Clair believed that each cat could recognize its own name.

A rustling noise came from the willows next to the fence. A fat orange tabby strode out, plump from the other rounds of late-night feedings it had in the area. It trotted unhurriedly to the front steps and paused there, waiting for Clair to back away from the dish. "That's a good kitty," she said softly to the cat. "Drink up, but save some for Thomas."

A scratching sound came from the flight of stairs to the cellar, the same stairs on which she had first met Danny. "That must be Thomas now," she remarked to Toodles. "Thomas, what are you doing down there? Come and drink your share before Toodles has it all."

But as quickly as the thin rustle started, it stopped again, and the dark stairs were silent. Clair could not see well into the depth because of the light that came from inside the entryway behind her.

"Thomas?" she inquired, rising and stepping forward from the door.

Thomas, her favorite of all, was an old gray cat reaching the end of his days. She began to worry that he might be hurt. Clair edged around Toodles, who was greedily slurping the milk, taking advantage of the absence of the other.

She pulled the door shut, walked down the three steps to the sidewalk, and stared blankly down the cellar stairs, waiting for her eyes to adjust to the light. The black iron gate swung open. She had taken the first step down when what sounded like a catfight erupted near her front door.

Evidently Thomas had arrived, demanding his share of the milk. And an unwilling Toodles was hissing and bristling at Thomas.

"Thomas! Toodles! Stop it at once," she commanded. "There's plenty to share."

Just then a pair of black-gloved hands clasped her head from behind and pushed her to her knees. She tried to scream, but one of the hands held her mouth and nose shut. The tiny sound that escaped was only a pathetic hum.

As Clair struggled to breathe, she scratched at her assailant.

An unfamiliar sickly sweet smell assaulted her senses. One gloved hand was rapidly swapped with the other, and the new grip held a wad of cotton soaked in the penetrating aroma.

Clair's eyes went wide. *Chloroform!* Her father had told her about it. It would knock her out! She must not breathe it in, yet she had to get air!

She was still on her knees, and the hand released her nose,

allowing her to draw in a new breath. But her head was clamped too tightly to turn away from the drug. Her eyes bulged, and her vision grew black and fuzzy. Before it went completely dark, she heard footsteps. Someone else was coming across the street in the night. . . .

•••

A second man crept across the street toward his partner and the girl victim. He carried a coil of rope that they bound the now-sleeping girl with. They used a handkerchief to gag her, in case she woke up.

By now the street was devoid of any other sound, except for the trotting of a horse-drawn carriage.

A carriage that stopped in front of the girl's house.

•••

Inspector Avery peered out the curtained window of the second-floor study in his home and toward the coach that had just arrived. It certainly was a dark night.

The inspector rose from his work to greet what he assumed would be a late-night caller. But as he reached the front hallway, he heard the clatter of the carriage pulling away.

Strange, he thought, rubbing his chin.

He opened the door to stare after the disappearing carriage . . . and scared the stray cats away from their saucer of milk.

Had the carriage simply come to the wrong address?

•••

It was late in the evening and a very dark night when Sherlock Holmes once again fetched Toby and the boys. As they listened to the latest kidnapping, they inhaled in shock. They had an even-more-personal stake involved in this search. Clair Avery had been kidnapped!

"I sure hope we find her," Duff said. "She's nice."

"From this point, the carriage departed," Holmes explained, standing in the street outside the Avery home. "With some of Clair's clothing, Toby should be able to track it sufficiently . . . if they have not done as last time."

Danny shuddered at the thought.

"Find, Toby, find," he said to the dog, waving a slipper in front of the dog's snout. "Go!"

Toby trotted to the middle of the street and sniffed around in a half circle. Danny imagined this arc to be where Clair's feet had swung over the pavement as the kidnappers hauled her to the carriage. Suddenly the dog selected his path, and the pursuit was on! The Baker Street Brigade and their leader ran to keep up.

The path that they followed was not confusing and zigzagged like the last, and Holmes appeared pleased that it was heading directly north. "They were in a great hurry to leave the scene," Holmes announced. "This may be the break we've been waiting for!"

When the trail reached the river, it turned and headed west to London Bridge. Once there they crossed over to the north side and then turned east again. There were no sidetracks, no wasted motion by Toby. It was as if the kidnappers wanted to leave a direct path clearly marked.

"Stop, Toby!" Holmes cried as they stopped for a short rest. "He is leading us to a definite point on the river. It could very well be that we will find the hideout tonight!"

"Let's not stop now!" Danny urged. "Can't we go faster?"

"You want to outrun old Toby?" Peachy teased. "Want to be her hero again?"

"We've got to find her!"

"Boys, boys!" Holmes said with a chuckle. "I see there is more to this than I had originally thought. A love triangle perhaps?"

"Aw, Danny's spooney," Peachy heckled.

"No," Danny volunteered to save them both the embarrassment. "We're just concerned, that's all."

As they set off down Lower Thames Street, they came in view of the Tower of London. Its huge stone walls loomed gray and shadowed in the night and echoed with the footsteps of the guards marching on their rounds inside.

Toby stopped and sniffed the air, then the ground all around everyone's feet.

"The area around the Tower is well trafficked by carriage and pedestrian alike," Holmes explained. "Indeed, this may be the criminals' first attempt to confuse any trackers."

Toby continued to sniff, then yelped and ran back in the direction from which the group had come.

"Oh no," Peachy said. "He's all confused now."

"Hold your assumptions until you have evidence to back them up," Holmes said. "I think you'll find we're on the opposite side of the road now."

Danny thought about that and realized he was right. "That means Toby's still on track, and the carriage turned around to travel the opposite direction on the correct side of the road."

"Right," Holmes agreed.

They traveled west on Upper Thames Street, then down Stew Lane to Queenhithe Dock. Danny knew that a water taxi could be hired here, and it was a place for private boats to put ashore passengers by way of small rowboats.

When Toby arrived there, he trotted down the steps to the water's edge, tracked around in a circle, then sat wagging his tail in the shallow water.

"No, no, no," Holmes said at last. "This will not do at all. They've taken a boat from here."

"But Toby could still track the carriage, couldn't he?" Danny offered as a solution. "Then at least we could arrest the driver."

"Toby could if we had a piece of the carriage, but the dog has the scent of Clair's slipper to follow, not the driver or a wagon wheel."

Holmes put a leash on Toby, and the group turned from the water. "I fear for the children," the master detective said. "The criminals we are dealing with here are of extraordinary caliber, not some ordinary London thugs." He paused and frowned. "The criminals behind these kidnappings are diabolically clever, and that may mean that their plan is fiendish as well. Yes, there is evil wit behind this caper, and it will take some deep thinking to understand it all."

●●●

Danny shifted restlessly on his cot in the open sleeping floor of the Ragged School and thought about Clair. Peachy and Duff sat at the foot of their beds, cleaning their muddy shoes. The three were alone within the blanket-partitioned space.

"Peachy," Danny said quietly. "Peachy, I was just thinking of Clair—I mean Clair's father. Shouldn't we try to do something for him?"

Peachy did not look up from his work. "Oh, concerned about her dad now, eh? Are you sure you don't just want to get in good with him?"

"Peachy," Danny snapped, annoyed by the way his friend teased. "Leave off, will you? That line of yours never was funny, and it isn't any better now."

Peachy dropped his shoes and leaped to his feet with fists clenched, ready to fight. Danny stood up quickly, his anger rising, and lunged. In an instant, the two boys were wrestling around on the floor, pulling hair and yelling insults, while Duff danced around the scrap, trying to pull them apart.

Peachy had rolled on top of Danny and was about to start swinging when he felt a big hand on his collar. He was picked up off of Danny, lifted to his tiptoes, and held there like a rag doll. Peachy managed to turn and glance at his captor, and found Duff's familiar face.

"Be nice," Duff said. "Be nice. And you too, Danny." He let go unexpectedly after delivering this reprimand.

Peachy landed hard on his backside on the bare wooden floor. He sat still, rubbing his throat where the collar had pressed into the flesh, and turned to look at Duff.

Duff was busy shining his shoes again, as if nothing at all had just taken place.

"Listen, Peachy," Danny said, standing up and extending his hand. "I didn't mean to snap, but I'm serious. I'm scared for Clair, and I think we should do something to cheer up her father. You remember how worried Clair was about him."

Peachy did not look up. "Sorry," he offered. "I'm scared for her, too, but I hide it by teasing, see? It's just . . . never mind." He paused, then added, "What can we do?"

"I've been thinking about that," Danny said. "You remember that picture we saw taken?" Peachy shook his head, as if losing track of what Danny was talking about. "You know—the one with Clair and the donkey and the monkey?"

"I remember," Duff volunteered. "The monkey was funny."

"Righto," Peachy agreed. "What about it?"

"I've been saving up some coppers, and I have sixpence set aside. Perhaps we could chip in and buy it for him. Just a shilling, the photographer said. What do you say?"

Before Peachy could answer, Headmaster Ingram walked over to where the boys sat and joined them. "I hear there's been some trouble between you lads. One of your neighbors was complaining about the noise. What seems to be the trouble?"

Danny looked at Peachy, who shook his head. "Me and Peachy were just having a bit of a discussion. We were wondering where that funny photographer's shop was. You know, the one that took the school picture for us?"

"Ah yes," Ingram said. "If I'm not mistaken, his shop is in Basinghall Street up in East Central. No. 5 or 6, if I'm correct. Are you sure that's all it was? No fight?"

Danny and Peachy shook their heads solemnly, and if Headmaster Ingram did not believe them completely, he did not press the matter.

As soon as the headmaster left, the boys made plans to travel to the shop the following morning and purchase the picture for Clair's father.

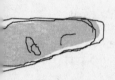

Nine

When London's morning came, crisp and clear, Danny, Duff, and Peachy set off to find the photographer's shop. The cold morning air relieved none of the alarm they felt at Clair's disappearance, though. Except for an occasional comment by Duff, the group was silent.

"Blimey, I'm hungry," Duff said, spouting a plume of steam from his breath. "We left without no prog!" But the other two did not respond, and soon Duff forgot his stomach. He returned to entertaining himself by exhaling deeply in rhythm, pretending he was a locomotive. He soon had examples to follow as his puffing was matched by the real thing when the group passed the tracks of London Bridge Station, filled with trains arriving from the suburbs.

There was only a slight chance that the shop would be open so early in the morning. But the boys had papers to sell later, and the early morning was the only time they would have free in their day to be so far from work and home.

"Can't be," Danny said suddenly aloud.

"What?" Peachy asked. He sounded annoyed and groggy. "What can't be?"

"I was thinking about Cap'n Mewsley. He can't be guilty. He was in prison when Clair was snatched. That's one piece of good news, eh?"

"Not too fast there, Danny," Peachy said. "He could still be part of a gang. They've still got the evidence of the stained fingers and the money. It all ties in. Don't you see?"

"I guess so," Danny said, sounding dejected again. "I just can't believe it's him doing all this and being back of taking Clair."

"Me neither. Just can't believe it," Duff said loudly. "He's a nice man."

"Well," Peachy scolded, "nice guys can be criminals, too."

Danny glared at Peachy, and the group walked on in silence again. Soon they found themselves in Basinghall Street, the location of the photographer's shop.

"There it is!" Peachy pointed down the lane to where a large sign, painted brown and shaped like a camera, hung above one of the old shops. The wavy glass in the bow window suggested that the building was at least a hundred years old.

When they arrived at the door, it appeared they were indeed too early. Drapes, once ivory colored but now stained with brown streaks and covered with dust and cobwebs, were drawn over the windows. A hand-lettered sign, confirming a later opening hour, was tacked to the door.

But as the group turned to leave, the entry to the shop swung open suddenly. "May I be of some service to you?" inquired a voice. They recognized the Turkish photographer, even without his monkey. "Are you looking for something in particular? A group portrait perhaps?"

Peachy spoke up. "We came to buy a picture, but it looked like you were closed."

"No, no, my friends," the man protested. "Please come in. I was just preparing for the day when I caught a glimpse of you outside."

The interior mirrored the neglect they had seen on the curtains. Uncorked brown bottles of chemicals sat on the floor, allowing their smelly contents to waft about freely in the tiny work space. The fumes alone could have stained the cloth in the window, but there was plenty of other dirt also. On one wall, a lone picture hung encased in a dusty oak frame. The image in the photo was too faded to make out anymore.

Piles of wooden photographic plates occupied the only two chairs and littered the top of a battered desk. The cubicle was otherwise empty, except for a narrow wooden counter across one end of the room, on which sat an old cash register. Behind the counter, on the back wall, a beaded doorway led into a space where the staircase to the upper floors was dimly visible.

"Woof," Duff said, sneezing. "This place smells worse than Cap'n Mewsley."

Peachy took the responsibility of elbowing Duff to silence him.

"Yes, yes. I am very sorry for that, my friend," apologized the photographer, flashing a crooked smile. "I do not usually have many customers in my humble shop here. Now about your picture . . . what shall it be?"

"Actually, we've come about the one you took a few days ago," Danny said, "of a girl about our age. You know, Clair Avery?"

"Yes, but of course," the man replied. "When you all took a liking to my monkey, yes?"

"That's the one," Danny said.

Duff smiled at the memory of the playful animal. "Where is it? Can I see?"

"Alas, I do not have it, I am so terribly sorry to report."

"You lost your monkey?" Duff said in a worried tone. "Was it stolen?"

"Pipe down, Duff," Peachy ordered. "Where is the photo then?"

"I regret to inform you, young sirs, that I do not have it," the man repeated, then paused while he looked around the bare room.

"You see, the glass on which the images appear is very fragile. I'm afraid my donkey jolted it far too much and did not keep it whole. Most unfortunate. Your friend is a most charming subject, yes?"

"That's too bad," Danny said. "It was meant to be a gift."

"Well, young sir, I will happily refund your money. After all, you do not pay for what you do not get, eh?" And he walked behind the counter to fetch a shilling from the brass cash register.

"Wait," Danny said.

Peachy rolled his eyes.

"We hadn't paid yet," Danny said. "You said she could pay when you brought it back."

"Oh, it is as you say. Well, here is for your honesty." With that, he tossed the coin to Peachy, who smiled, then pocketed the loot. "I am a nice man, eh? Maybe you will buy a picture some other day."

The group left the stale-smelling shop of mixed sharp and musty odors. "Smells like a tanning yard in there," Peachy complained. "I wouldn't want to stay inside too long."

"It's too bad we couldn't get the picture," Danny fretted.

"Ah, cheer up then," Peachy urged. "At least we got something out of it."

"He really is a nice man," Duff observed.

When they left the photographer's shop, at last the sun was up enough to warm the temperature of the air. The day was growing more pleasant.

●●●

The boys walked aimlessly for a time after they left the shop, not knowing what to do, not knowing if they could help at all.

"What use are we?" Peachy asked. "We can't find a scent, can't even cheer someone up. Seems like we're more in the way of this investigation than helping it at all."

"But we have to keep trying. Cap'n Mewsley is depending on us, and somewhere, so is Clair. If we don't keep trying and something bad happens to Clair, we'll hate ourselves forever."

"But that's no help, Danny! I know we have to do something,

but what? Maybe we should look for clues under Mr. Holmes's sofa. Maybe we should sail down the Nile and look for them there. Maybe we can just ask Duff here. Oy, Duff! Do you know where to find clues?"

Duff scowled at Peachy and breathed hard, formulating the words he would say and growing angrier as he thought. "You are not nice right now. I do not like not-nice people." He clasped a thick muscular hand on the back of Peachy's neck, and Peachy flinched underneath it. "I like you better when you are nice. So be." His grip slacked, and they walked on.

"What do you suggest we do, Danny?" Peachy asked at last, his voice squeaking from the pressure still on his neck.

Duff took his hand off Peachy's neck. He could tell his friend was now trying hard to speak nicely.

"The manhole cover again," Danny said. "Let's go to the last real clue we had. After all, it's not far."

"Great!" Peachy said sarcastically. "Let's just go looking every place we've already . . ."

Duff glared at him, and Peachy stopped suddenly.

"Sure, Danny," Peachy said quickly. "Let's go back to the sewer."

Duff stopped walking and dropped from the middle of the trio. "Nope. No sewer. Rats is in sewers, and I don't like rats."

"No, listen, Duff," Danny said. "It'll be all right."

"There's rats in every sewer. Just you can't see 'em all the time."

Danny sighed. "All right then. Can you find your way back to Mr. Holmes? You can tell him what we are . . . no," he corrected himself, "just tell him that we have nothing to report. Have you got that?"

"Got that. Nothin' to report. I can find that place with my eyes open if I have to."

Danny and Peachy laughed and sent Duff on his way.

Duff stopped long enough to peer back at his friends as they continued toward the manhole near the Palace Hotel, a block away.

•••

Peachy and Danny arrived at the manhole cover in the place where Toby had lost the scent. The location suggested nothing suspicious or unusual. The rear of the respectable Palace Hotel was a short distance away, and the boys knew that the shop of the strange but harmless photographer was only another block over.

Danny wondered if this expedition was a colossal waste of time. He squatted down, tugging at the heavy steel lid. "Give me a hand with this thing."

He looked up at Peachy. Peachy was turning his head from side to side—evidently to see if anyone was watching. Finally he bent down to help Danny lift.

"On the count of three," Danny said. "One, two, three . . ."

The boys grunted with the strain. At first it seemed that the cover was stuck tight. Then slowly it began to inch upward on one side. Warm air gushed out from the tiny crack.

Their fingers turned white at the knuckles from the weight. Tipping the circular lid up on one side, the thick disk neared its fully open position, revealing a gaping black hole leading down.

"Danny, look! There's a ladder," Peachy said with excitement.

"You climb down," Danny instructed. "I'll hold the cover."

Peachy sat on the edge of the chasm and cautiously placed one foot on the uppermost rung, testing it with his weight. Then he began his descent into the inky darkness.

Danny stood over the hole, balancing the cover between his knees and watching the last glimpse of Peachy's red hair disappear in the gloom.

Peachy called up from the depths, "I'm at the bottom."

"What's down there?"

"It's not a sewer or a drain after all. It's some kind of a tunnel filled with pipes."

"Where does it go?" Danny asked.

"One way is all dark, but there's a light from the other direction. I think that's where all the warm air is coming from."

"How far away is the light?"

Peachy's voice echoed up from below. "I can't tell, but I think it's toward the Palace Hotel."

Danny raised his head in the direction of the hotel. He could see the flat, windowless expanse of its back wall and a tangle of heating and ventilation pipes that climbed it.

"Peachy, I'm coming down." With the weight of the metal manhole cap resting against his back, Danny climbed down to the third rung. When he ducked suddenly, the steel cap came crashing down. The reverberations were so loud in the confined space that Danny thought they would knock him off the ladder. He clung to the rungs until the clanging echoes stopped. . . . Even then his ears were still ringing.

A sudden unpleasant thought struck Danny, and he stood upright. Pushing up hard with his head and hands, he exclaimed, "Oh, blimey!"

"What's wrong?" Peachy asked.

"The cap. I think it's stuck."

"Well, come on then. If we can't go back up and the other tunnels are dark, then there's only one way to go," Peachy concluded.

Was his friend really as unconcerned as he sounded? Danny wondered. "I can't see," he complained. "Where am I going?"

"Don't worry. You'll see the light when you get to the bottom," Peachy said. "Just stop coming for a second while I crawl out of your way. Or else you'll be setting a boot on my head."

Danny could hear the scuffling noises as Peachy moved from beneath him. Reaching the bottom of the ladder, Danny squatted low, feeling the curved ceiling of the pipe with one hand and catching hold of Peachy's foot with the other. The glimmer of light coming from one direction revealed Peachy's back and an overhead cluster of pipes and tubes.

Something besides Peachy's breathing also reached his ears. "Listen, can you hear that?" Danny asked. He heard voices—a long way off and very faint.

"That's outside," Peachy replied. "Come on."

"No, wait. Put your ear to the pipe."

Peachy did as Danny said. "Too soft. I can't understand what they're saying."

"Neither can I," Danny fired back. "But someone else is down here!"

The pair crawled on. Flat on their bellies, they pulled themselves along by their elbows and pushed with their toes. Danny looked up past Peachy's shoulders to check the progress. For a long time, the light seemed no nearer. Then, finally, the gleam grew until Danny could see that the tube through which they crawled opened out just ahead.

The tunnel faced a surface of white stone, but between the opening and the wall was a drop-off. Danny squeezed up alongside Peachy, who was already peering over the edge.

Since they had already descended about twenty feet below the street, the additional empty space below startled Danny. Another twenty or twenty-five feet straight down separated them from a stone floor.

On the flat expanse below, Danny could see two cartlike trash bins, several industrial-sized piles of laundry, and a steaming boiler. Trickles of water filled the grout of the red-stained tiles and dampened most of the floor.

"Would you take a squint at all this?" Danny said with astonishment. "This has got to be below the hotel. I wonder if they know about this way in."

Danny and Peachy exchanged a worried look. At least one other person knew about this tunnel. What if the escaping kidnapper had not come this way by chance but had known about this route all along?

"Did you hear that?" Peachy asked in a hushed tone.

"The voices again. This time louder."

The boys listened intently, hearing the screeching complaint of metal on metal. It was loud, almost as if it were right next to them. Then a wheeled bin rolled across the floor, crashing into the pipes below their niche.

The unexpected collision rattled Danny's brain. It seemed that in this steamy underworld, things were always either too loud or too quiet, never in between.

"Ouch," Danny cried, covering his throbbing ears. Peachy hurriedly thrust one palm over Danny's mouth and pointed downward with the other hand.

A dark-skinned man walked out from a corridor and entered the narrow space below them. He looked around as if searching for something or someone. Could he have heard Danny's cry?

The figure walked past the boiler to the far corner of the room, checking behind it. After finding nothing, he left the room again by climbing a flight of stairs. Danny and Peachy had not seen the stairs before, but now they could just make out some steps against the far wall.

They listened intently as the man clunked his way up the wooden treads. A door slammed. Then silence filled the room once more.

"That was a bit close for me," Danny whispered, blinking at Peachy.

"Too right. Good thing he's gone," Peachy agreed. "But that don't solve our problem. How are we gonna get out of here?"

The boys rested with their heads poking out of the opening, pondering the depth and the distance below them. After Danny had searched from ceiling to floor, he muttered, "Looks like we're going to have to climb down the pipes."

"Climb down the pipes! We're at least twenty feet off the ground!" Peachy exclaimed. "How're we supposed to do that?"

"Hang on tight, I guess," Danny said dryly. "The kidnapper must have done it, and so can we."

"What if that bloke comes back while we're still hanging out there?" Peachy argued.

Danny shrugged. "We'll just have to chance it. We got no other choice."

"I'll go first then," Peachy insisted. "That way I won't knock you off, too, when I fall!"

Holding tight to the pipes, Peachy crawled out of the hole, trembling over the brink of the drop-off. Danny saw that his friend's hands were shaking. In front of Peachy stretched an iron beam that bridged the space, reaching across to a support pillar on the wall opposite. Peachy wrapped his arms around the beam and, closing his eyes, scooted his legs out over the edge.

Peachy seemed to hang from the beam like a towel over a rack. Dangling from his arms, he swayed from side to side.

Danny leaned out to encourage him. "It's easy. Just keep looking at me and don't look down."

Peachy concentrated. Steadying himself, he curled his legs around a bunch of rusty wet pipes. But when he tried to transfer his grip from the beam to the pipes, he missed and began to lean dangerously backward. His weight was supported only by his legs and a fingertip hold on the slippery metal.

"Peachy, hold on!" Danny cried, reaching out to help.

"Don't let me fall, Danny!" Peachy begged.

"Take my hand!"

With his arm outstretched to Danny's, Peachy's hand trembled. Barely touching, their fingers brushed, then twined together. Danny pulled hard, elevating his body once more until Peachy had one hand on the lip of the ledge. With the other he still clung to the upright tubes. Water ran down Peachy's forearm, then dripped from his elbow to the ground. Peachy clung there, frozen with fear.

"Peachy, look at me," Danny whispered calmly. "You'll be all right. All you have to do is slide down now." Peachy's eyes were closed. Speechless and rigid, he could not move.

"Loosen your grip, Peachy," Danny told him softly. "All you have to do is slide down, and you'll be okay."

Peachy's eyes blinked open, focusing on Danny. Slowly, one finger at a time, Peachy loosened his grip. His fingertips and the soles of his shoes squeaked on the damp metal surface, but he gently slid downward, splashing safely to the ground.

"Good job, mate," Danny congratulated. "I know how you hate heights."

"Thank you," Peachy said quietly.

"I wasn't gonna let you fall."

"Thanks," Peachy said again with a drawn-out sigh. Then he slapped his hands on his filthy, rust-covered legs and said, "Now it's your turn."

Danny shimmied out on the beam. He waited, suspended for a moment, until his swaying stopped. Next he pulled himself hand by hand until his feet reached the rods. He clenched them tight with his legs and slid down with the speed and skill of an experienced fireman.

The expansive height in the area over the pipes gave way to a low-ceilinged room from which hung large hooks locked into a network of tracks. Piles of sheets, towels, and table linen were heaped all over the floor, and more sacks filled with more laundry hung about the ceiling, suspended from the hooks.

Danny pushed one of the white bags, and the rollers above resisted a bit before allowing the sack to move. It slid along the track, then stopped and swung back and forth.

"Nothing very mysterious about a laundry," Peachy said. "Let's go before they catch us here and make us wash clothes."

"But the man who attacked Clair had to come through here," Danny reminded him. "Let's not give up yet."

The room was filled with steam, let off at intervals by the huge boiler that sat against one wall, making the room humid and uncomfortably warm. Near the boiler were large vats of sudsy water bubbling and stewing with sheets. Hot water was fed into the tanks by a maze of pipes. The vats were so large that each had steps and a platform around the rim. Wooden paddles leaned against the washtubs, showing how the linen was scrubbed.

Danny heard a faint noise much like the hissing of the boiler but growing into a louder rumble. It came from the direction of the stairs. "What's that?" he asked Peachy.

"I don't know, but we'd better hide."

The two friends jumped behind the largest heap of full laundry sacks, just behind the stairs. The hissing sound grew still louder, and

Danny realized it was coming from above them. Just as he looked up, another large bag of soiled tablecloths plunged into view from a laundry chute over his head. It bounced off the top of the pile, somersaulted, and smothered Danny underneath it. Struggling to move the bag, Danny heard Peachy let out a snorting laugh.

"Ha-ha," Danny said, glaring at Peachy as he fought his way free and sat up. "Very funny. You just wait until . . ." The sliding sound came again, and both Danny and Peachy scrambled clear of the pile an instant before another heavy bag dropped.

Moving about the room again, they examined all the big equipment. Near the boiler were large hand-cranked mangles, big machines with rollers for wringing out the laundry after it came sopping from the wash. Next to them were huge wooden racks, used for drying the linen after it was wrung out. On the other side of the room were great steam presses for flattening out all the wrinkles in the sheets.

"Sure is impressive," Danny said. "A lot of big equipment."

Peachy nodded as he examined the wall behind the presses. A big pile of ripped and torn damp sheets was heaped there, covered in mildew and rust stains. "Looks like these have been here since good Queen Bess. Phew! They stink!"

"This wall . . . did you notice it's different?" Danny pointed out. "It isn't brick like the rest. Could it be that—?" Danny had not finished when they heard more noises from over their heads—the slam of a door and footsteps on the staircase. "Quick, back to hiding!" They dashed behind the pile of sacks under the laundry chute once more.

The boys were afraid to rise for fear of being seen. But they caught a glimpse of the man's legs and sandaled feet as he passed inches away. Could it be the bloke Danny had chased from the market before he'd gotten a knock on the head?

The man disappeared in the direction of the wall that Danny and Peachy had been examining. A long time passed while Danny listened intently. What was the man doing? How long would they have to remain hidden?

There was the sound of something heavy being dragged across the floor, followed by the unmistakable noise of ripping cloth. That was followed by an angry voice speaking phrases in a foreign tongue that could only be curses. Then there was silence.

Danny looked at Peachy in the stillness. Had the man really gone, or had he heard the boys somehow and was waiting for them to emerge from hiding?

Finally Danny got up his nerve and rose to peek over the stack of linen. "Peachy," he whispered, "there's a door on that wall!"

The man had moved the moldy mass of laundry and gone through the hidden opening.

A heavy clank of metal scared the boys into ducking down again.

"Take another look," Peachy urged when no one reappeared and everything remained quiet.

"No!" Danny protested. "You go." Finally they rose together and looked. The door stood open and led into a dimly lit second room. The interior of the previously secret room was a disappointment, though. It was empty, except for the potbellied shape of another boiler or furnace—dark and obviously not in use. The chamber itself was completely plain, other than a single row of lighter-colored tile that decorated the drab brick wall. But for the room to be empty . . .

"He's gone!" Danny exclaimed. "But where . . . ?"

"Come on, Danny," Peachy urged. "Maybe we won't get another chance to clear off!"

"But where did he go?"

"Maybe he's in the boiler," Peachy joked.

Danny ran into the back room and cranked the circular iron wheel that operated the steel door. To his dismay, it refused to budge. "Must be rusted solid," Danny groaned. "He couldn't have gone in there!"

"Fair enough and good riddance to him! We have mysteries in plenty without getting our necks wrung for another one. Let's get out of here!"

And Peachy pulled the still-protesting Danny back to the laundry area and up the steps.

•••

When they came to the top, Peachy dropped to his stomach on the landing. Slowly he pushed open a door and found he was looking into a hallway that connected to the lobby of what had to be the Palace Hotel. A potted palm partly concealed the opening.

From where Peachy lay, he could see the large chrome-and-glass revolving door that served as an entrance to the hotel. The lobby was not busy, which Peachy at first thought was good, before he realized that it would make their escape more noticeable.

One bored clerk was on duty at the front desk, and he appeared to be dozing off. Peachy smiled at the row of potted trees and bushes that marched in rank down the wall toward the street exit.

"All right, Danny," he hissed. "Follow me." Peachy crawled out from under the rope and moved to his right behind the first of the plants. He looked back to the stairs where Danny was still sitting, either afraid to move or lost in thought. Peachy motioned angrily for him to follow, and Danny's head jerked as if he were just waking up. Peachy mouthed the words *"come on."*

Danny left his hiding place and crawled to the first plant just as Peachy lunged to the second. They moved in this way all around the empty lobby until there were no more plants to conceal them. When Danny reached the last plant next to Peachy, he said, "What do we do now? Just walk out?"

"No, watch me." Peachy stood up suddenly with his back toward the exit.

"Hey, you kids!" shouted the clerk, looking up from the newspaper he was reading. "You're not allowed in here! You just march right back out the way you came in."

Danny nearly walked back to the stairs to the basement, but Peachy grabbed him and hauled him to the door. Once outside Peachy laughed. "That dumb bloke thought we was sneaking *in!*

Whew, what a close one." Every step away from the hotel made them feel safer.

"Peachy," Danny said, "something's not right. The whole investigation is taking too long. I don't know if we're any closer to finding Clair and the other kids, but that man down there, he was definitely wearing sandals like the bloke the other day. And that language he spouted. It might be . . ."

"Egyptian. Arabic. Who knows?" Peachy finished. "So what?"

"Well, I think if you talked to Cap'n Mewsley, he might be able to help. He knows about the Nile . . . and well, I got this hunch. So if you go do that, I'll see Mr. Holmes and tell him what we found out here."

So they split up. Danny went to Baker Street, and Peachy headed for Newgate Prison.

Ten

Danny ran through the busy streets, thinking about the strange disappearance of the man in the subterranean room. He wondered about the secret destination hidden somewhere deep inside the structure. What did it all mean? Was it connected to the kidnappings and the whereabouts of Clair, or had they struck some new mystery?

He was a little nervous of Sherlock Holmes's reaction to their unauthorized snooping. Danny could not be sure if the detective would be happy or upset with the work they had done. Were they really investigating or just letting their imaginations race ahead of the facts? As he rounded the corner of Marylebone Road and turned onto Baker Street, Danny wondered what Holmes would say.

At 221B, the outside door was locked this time. Danny rapped loudly on the panel, and it opened a split second later. Danny jumped back at the suddenness with which it was answered.

"Aha!" Holmes exclaimed. "I knew it was you! Come in, Wiggins." The detective was again dressed in his rubber workshop apron, long gauntlets, and goggles.

"But how could you know it was . . . ?" Danny tried to ask, but Holmes was already taking the stairs back to his study two risers at a time.

"No time to chat, Wiggins! I'm in the middle of an important experiment."

Danny removed his cap, closed the door behind him, and followed Holmes up the stairs. When he reached the landing, he detected a now-familiar foul odor in the air.

"Impressive, isn't it?" Holmes asked. But Danny couldn't answer. He simply stared at the array of glass bottles and beakers, three times as many as on the earlier visit, interconnected by a network of stoppers and hoses. Multiple gas burners were heating different parts of the assembly. Danny heard the gurgle of boiling liquid as it pushed its way through the flasks, condensers, retorts, and tubing. Some beakers were filled with green, some with a dingy brown. He wondered how he could interrupt the detective's concentration to deliver his report.

"Mr. Holmes," Danny began.

"Shhh!" Holmes scolded. "I'm coming to the end of it. Watch! I can prove that Miles, the dynamiter, constructed a bomb while in prison! He used soap flakes, candle wax, kerosene, and sugar—all easily available. Only the acid had to be smuggled in!" Holmes walked around the table to where a turnip-shaped flask with a spigot at the bottom was held up by metal rods.

From what Danny could tell, the two different-colored liquids ended up here, by means of two glass tubes that entered the top of the flask. Absorbed in spite of himself, Danny moved forward to lean on the table.

"Don't touch that!" Holmes erupted, and Danny jumped. "I have small amounts of sulfuric acid all over my work space. No doubt you've smelled it?"

Danny nodded.

"Well, it will burn your skin, staining your hands a dirty yellow. It could even injure you severely if you are in contact too long."

Holmes continued with his work, collecting a flat glass petri dish from a cupboard and placing it under the spout. With a precise motion of his gloved hand on the spigot, three drops fell, spattering in the dish. "Now I'll put the lid back on it, and we'll examine it when it's cool." With his attention finally undivided, Holmes gave Danny a chance to explain his visit.

But something was also bubbling in Danny's head. "It smells like the photographer's shop in here."

"That is to be expected, Wiggins. Photographers use the same acid in the production of their plates. What photographer's shop?"

"When Peachy and I first met Clair, she had her picture taken on a donkey by the same photographer who took our school photo. She thought it would cheer up her father. The man said he would bring it back to her house when it was done. When Clair was kidnapped, Peachy and I thought we should get it for her father anyway, so we found out where the shop was and went there."

Holmes stripped off the rubber gloves and tossed them on the floor, then pushed the goggles up onto his forehead. "And did the man have the picture on hand?" Holmes sat down and listened attentively to Danny's reply.

"No, as a matter of fact, he said it was broken."

"Wiggins, you may have stumbled onto something very, very important." Holmes rose from his chair and took off the apron. "Come, boy, we must go to this shop."

"But that's not what I came here to tell you," Danny protested. "I wanted to tell you that Toby tracked the man from Leadenhall Market to a spot in the East End. When we got to the end of the trail, the man I chased had apparently gone down a sewage drain cover. But the drain turned out not to be a drain at all."

Holmes looked up sharply. Danny told him about the man disappearing while he and Peachy were hidden in the laundry area and about the abandoned boiler that was the only thing visible in the hidden room they found. He also explained that the end of their exploration brought them up from the basement of the Palace Hotel.

"Wiggins, where is the photographer's shop?"

"Over in the East End. About a block from the hotel. Why?"

"No time to explain! Your work has produced a more serious result than I could have first imagined! We must enlist other help, and there is no time to lose! I've been so blind! Wait here! Attempt nothing on your own." With that he grabbed his cane and hat and hurried to the street below.

•••

Although Peachy was on his way to visit Cap'n Mewsley in Newgate Prison, he wasn't very optimistic about his chances of getting in. And he was even less hopeful that the ramblings of their friend could somehow help to unravel the mystery.

When Peachy arrived at the prison, he saw the families of inmates on the street outside, hoping for a chance to see a prisoner. Very few relatives were allowed into the jail itself unless they had good reason. Without the written request by Sherlock Holmes, which had gotten them access the first time, Peachy did not think he had a chance.

Once across the street, Peachy looked the place up and down for a way in. Approaching the gate was another guard, leading a crying woman who was in turn leading three young boys. It appeared they were being allowed inside.

"Right this way, ma'am," he heard the guard say. In a flash of inspiration, Peachy lowered his head, joined the end of the line of children, conjured up some sobbing noises, and followed the group through the gate.

"When?" the woman asked the guard. "When did he go?"

"Last night, ma'am, in his cell. We've not moved him yet. He's still lying on his bunk." When she heard that, the woman let out a large wail, and the tears poured freely from her eyes. The other guards in the entry gate turned their eyes away as the bereaved party passed through.

It worked. The group was led to an inner building and down a long staircase where the darkness deepened and the moaning of prisoners grew louder.

When they reached the bottom of the staircase, Peachy ducked out from behind the family group and headed down the corridor toward Mewsley's cell. He knew he would have to move quickly.

Mewsley sat on a crate in his cell with the dim light from the holes above filtering around him. A group of men were gathered around him on the floor and listening intently as he spoke. "So there she was, the princess Tangili in all her splendor. She walked down the row of us that kneeled on the floor and patted the heads of the prisoners she would have executed for examples. At each touch they were hauled off screamin' to their doom. When she came to me—"

"Cap'n Mewsley!" Peachy called through the bars on the cell door. "It's me, Peachy."

Mewsley rose from his seat and walked to the grate. The crowd groaned almost in unison as their story was interrupted.

"Danny and me have found some things that may lead to the real kidnappers," Peachy told Cap'n Mewsley quickly. "But we don't know how it all fits, and we thought . . . well, we thought perhaps you know more than you think you do. What got you in trouble with the law before? But hurry, and tell me quick. I'm not supposed to be here."

"Your Mr. Holmes has me done up proper, I'm afeard. His word and my past sins come back to haunt me. All right, here's my story: You see, back in the Sudan, we were stranded in the desert for a long period with hardly any food and only murky pools of hot desert water to keep up alive. But I kept the men under control when they wanted to mutiny and head back to the river. I said, 'No, men. Captain Avery knows what he's about.'"

"Captain Avery?" Peachy interrupted. "Not the same Avery as the police inspector?"

"The very same. So, like I was saying, they wanted to mutiny, but I said no. And sure enough, they listened, and we marched back with no trouble. But I couldn't hold 'em for long without no better grub. There was chickens so close in the city, I could hear 'em squawkin' all the time as if to taunt me. So one night, I just decided to go and get us one for me and my mess mates. Worse luck! That old rooster made such a ruckus that I was caught with him right in the yard of the house from where I took it from. That olive trader, Caravaldi, had plenty and to spare, him bein' a right well-off merchant and all, but he would see me punished for tryin' to take his measly chicken. So I was put away in a little hot shack with no food or water and the sweatin' thinnin' me out to skin and bones. . . ."

By now the crowd of prisoners had gathered behind Mewsley at the bars to listen to the new story. Something was stirring in Peachy's head, but he could not quite grasp it. A connection was there, a connection that was barely out of reach. It was . . .

"Ahhh, wait!" Peachy shouted. "I've got it! Caravaldi—he was one of the people who had his child stolen. Well, so was Avery! You mean to tell me that they were in the Sudan together? Cappy, that's the connection! It must be!" He was proud of himself for figuring it out.

"They were in Africa together, so somebody's takin' their children for it? What does it all mean? How can it get me out of here?"

"It's a start! Mr. Holmes has to hear this! Don't give up, Cap'n. The truth is on the way!"

As Peachy ran off back up the corridor, he heard Mewsley continue his tale to the other prisoners.

•••

Though Danny reclined in Holmes's favorite chair by the small fireplace, he was anxious for the detective's return. What had made the investigator rush off in such a hurry? Where was he now? Did Peachy get in to see Mewsley? And where was Duff?

As Danny thought about all the particulars in the case, the sound of running feet reached him from the stairs. Without knocking, Peachy opened the door and burst into the room. "Mr. Holmes!" he yelled. "I've found the connection!"

Danny bolted upright out of the chair and into Peachy's view.

"Danny!" Peachy exclaimed. "It's you. Good! Where's Mr. Holmes? I've found the connection. I—"

"Wait, slow down, Peachy. Mr. Holmes has gone to the photographer's shop, and I told him about the hotel. Now what connection? What did Cap'n Mewsley tell you?"

"The families whose children have been kidnapped . . . I think they were all in the Sudan together. Well, maybe not together, but at the same time in the same place, you see?"

"That's it? They were in Africa at the same time? But that can't be it! That makes it look *worse* for Cap'n Mewsley, not better!"

"But don't you see? Not just that they were in the Sudan, but their *reason* for being there. All we need to know is what they were doing, and we'll know if they made the same enemies."

Danny was beginning to understand his theory. "Well, what *were* they there for?"

"Mewsley was in the army, even if he wasn't ever really a captain. Inspector Avery was in the army. Caravaldi was an olive-oil merchant . . . Cappy told me."

"But what were they all there for?" Danny wondered aloud. "Who are the others? You know, like the first kidnapping."

Peachy and Danny both dove into the pile of newspapers that littered the floor of the detective's study. They dug through past issues, leading back to the date of the original abductions.

"Here it is!" Danny exulted. "Thank goodness Mr. Holmes won't let Mrs. Hudson touch anything in here!"

"Dom-wahh-mule?" Peachy tried to pronounce the French name. "What does it say? Was he in Africa?"

"An arms dealer in the war!" Danny said triumphantly. "A merchant who . . . the war!" he exclaimed suddenly.

"The war brought all those people to the Sudan. And what was the war about?"

Peachy shrugged.

"Antislavery."

"But what would make someone take revenge over the antislavery movement?" Peachy wondered out loud.

"The Mahdists," Danny stated with confidence. "Remember? Cap'n Mewsley told us about those people whose sons were executed by General Gordon! Somehow all these families go back to the Mahdi and his revenge!"

"Right! Cappy even said they were still after revenge. So all the people who were there were against slavery. Wait, Danny, I think you're right. Quick, find the ransom note that Mr. Holmes showed us."

The two quickly scoured all the messages that lay strewn about the parlor and came up with a stack of the kidnappers' demands. Danny read the top one out loud.

"We have your child. Your child will be killed if you do not comply with our modest demands. Proof that your child is still alive will follow in the form of a photograph. Leave one hundred pounds in the designated location when the next set of instructions arrives with the photo. Leave the area and tell no one, or your child will be killed." A photo of a sobbing little boy in a cage fluttered to the floor.

"Danny, did you hear that?" Peachy asked. "The way the nose used the word *modest*? It sounds just like Mahdist!"

But Danny was no longer listening. He had bent down to retrieve the photo and was studying it intently.

"Did you hear me?" Peachy repeated. "It sounds the same."

"Peachy," Danny said, pointing to the photo with a trembling finger. "Don't look at the cage or the rope or the boy. Look at the wall. That row of tiles."

Peachy caught it instantly. "It's the same as in the hidden room below the hotel! So there is a connection somehow!"

"Right! Let's go and take these with us to show Mr. Holmes."

"To which? The shop or the hotel?" There was a moment of hesitation.

"It doesn't matter now! We'll decide as we go!"

Eleven

Danny and Peachy were stopped short when they neared the top of Basinghall Street. Policemen were keeping anyone from getting within two blocks of the photographer's shop, and already a crowd was beginning to form at the barricade in order to see what was going on.

"Crushers," Peachy said, shaking his head. "It's not supposed to work like this. They'll be the ones that end up tipping 'em off."

"I know," Danny agreed. "But by my guess, that's not far off from what Mr. Holmes wants."

They watched as two groups of policemen gathered on either side of the photo-shop door, while Inspector Avery stood poised to knock. He glanced from side to side, and at a nod of readiness from each of the groups, he banged heavily on the door. "Yakimans, open the door! We know who you really are, Ahmed Bashir! This is the Metropolitan Police. Open up!"

To the boys' and Inspector Avery's surprise, the door slowly creaked open under the blows of his fist.

For a moment all were silent as they stared expectantly at the now-open doorway for someone to emerge. A ripple of laughter ran through the crowd and was even shared by the boys and several of the bobbies. Instead of a dangerous criminal, a screeching monkey scampered out of the shop and ran up Avery's leg to perch on his head.

"You chaps, get serious!" Avery yelled as he stumbled backward while prying the creature's grip from around his neck.

The policemen advanced toward the shop. A dark brown bottle was hurled from an upstairs window. It narrowly missed hitting the inspector, then shattered on the pavement. From it swirled a murky yellow puddle that hissed on the cobblestones, instantly bleaching them pale white. Noxious fumes reached the noses of the men, making them back suddenly away.

Up the street Danny smelled it, too, recognizing it as the same odor as in Holmes's makeshift laboratory, but apparently in a much more concentrated form.

"Acid!" came a shout from the crowd. The policemen were no longer so eager to push forward.

"Come on!" shouted Avery, while folding a handkerchief to hold over his nose and mouth. "That means they are here!" He stepped over the acid on the cobblestones and led the men in through the doorway.

A minute later, a policeman cried out in pain and ran from the building, clutching and wiping his face. Apparently more glass vials of acid were being thrown inside the building.

"These rotters play tough," Peachy shouted in dismay.

As they watched, the man spattered in the face knelt and buried his head in a fountain. The sounds of angry voices and a great struggle came from inside the shop.

"Come on," Danny yelled as he grabbed Peachy by the arm. They elbowed through the crowd and ducked under the now-unmanned barricades. All the officers had gone to join the siege.

When they reached the door, they found the officers mingling around the tiny interior in bewilderment. In the middle of them was Avery, angrily questioning his men.

"What do you mean you don't know where he went? Didn't anyone see where the blackguard has gone? He was just in the back room, right before he hurled the last bottle of acid. Where is he now?"

An officer tramped down the stairs to report. "All clear, sir. No sign of him at all."

"Listen!" Danny froze with his ear turned toward the back room. "Can you hear that?" It was when he spoke up that the officers finally noticed the boys' presence on the scene.

"What're you doing in here?" Avery demanded.

"Wait," Danny said, "can't you hear it?" At Avery's command, the group fell silent, and then the sound was plain. A rumble and squeaking noise came from inside the back room. The bobbies surged through the doorway and fell silent again.

It sounded like a great wagon wheel turning slowly while in the distance a hundred horses trod on soft ground. "From that back wall!" Avery shouted. "There must be a secret panel. Find it!" Peachy and Danny both joined in the search, digging their fingers into any conspicuous seams in the wall and pulling with all their might.

Across the room on the opposite wall, an officer grabbed on to the stem of a gas lamp, apparently breaking it when it pulled downward. Directly in front of Peachy, a false panel moved back about an inch. Peachy kicked it hard, and it swung inward, revealing a cylindrical room about the size of a broom closet. It was completely dark and seemed empty. But now the rumbling noise poured out of the opening, filling the shop with the sound.

The officers came from all parts of the house and pushed and shoved their way forward to see the passageway. As their eyes adjusted to the darkness within, it appeared to be a well, falling deeply into the ground below.

"Look!" Peachy shouted. "A man, there!" As the crowd of officers jostled forward again to see inside, Peachy was bumped, lost his balance, and fell.

Before anyone could jump after him, another panel slid across the opening between the shop floor and the descending platform. Peachy was cut off!

"Get axes and rope," Avery commanded. "We'll chop our way through and lower ourselves down."

"Inspector," Danny cut in, "I think I know of a better way."

●●●

Peachy hit his head in the fall to the platform and was knocked unconscious. He gradually awoke to a girl's voice calling his name from far off in the distance. For an instant he thought he was dreaming.

"Oh, Peachy, you've had a nasty bump. Are you all right?" the girl asked.

Peachy tried to focus his eyes, but the light in the room was too dim and he was still dizzy. Then he recognized the voice. "Clair? Where are we?" he asked.

He tried to sit up but found he was restrained by the wrists. He was shackled to an iron cage, and Clair was inside it.

"We're in some sort of basement. I don't know where. They blindfolded me on the way here."

As Clair explained, Peachy suddenly remembered where "here" was and all the other events of the day. "We're in the basement of the photographer's shop. You know, the one that took your picture with the monkey?" He told her all about what had previously occurred on the street and how the criminal now had a name: Ahmed Bashir. He also told her about the connection he had found between all of the children who were kidnapped.

Clair pointed out of the bars over Peachy's shoulder. Other cages, each with a single occupant, were suspended nearby. Peachy saw the row of tile on the wall that he had noticed in the photograph and in the secret room.

The other children, all boys, were sitting quietly in their hanging cells, except for one. Clair gestured to a small boy who sat gazing at his feet, sucking his thumb, and sobbing against a small stuffed bear. He was the first kidnapped and the youngest, she explained.

"That's little Joseph," Clair said. "He won't eat, won't move. Just sits there crying all day and night."

"How long's he been that way?"

"I don't know," she said. "He was already like that when I got here."

"Poor little bloke, he'll starve to death if Mr. Holmes don't—" Peachy stopped short for fear that a guard might hear him.

"Doesn't what?" Clair asked.

Peachy looked around. "If Mr. Holmes don't find the way in here double-quick and get us out," he whispered. "That's what he's trying to do right now."

Clair gave a tiny hopeful smile and hugged Peachy through the bars. The cage swung, making the chain creak.

"What is that?" a voice yelled. "What are you doing?" Ahmed Bashir, once the funny photographer, stalked from behind a stack of crates. He walked toward them carrying a knobbed wooden club. "I said, what are you doing?" He was no longer the nice accommodating man who had given the boys money for nothing. He now seemed twice as big and impossibly mean, and he stared straight at Peachy.

"I was just waking up. I looked around too fast," Peachy replied.

The man walked up and checked the chain where Peachy's hands were tied to the bars.

"You are not to be looking around at all!" Bashir insisted. He swung his club down full force on the cage.

Clair screamed.

Peachy jumped, yanking the shackles cruelly into his wrists.

"It will not be long now, my pets," Bashir said in a louder, evil voice. "Soon you will be going to your new homes. Now if any of you infidel toads have some looking to do, let it be at your feet like little Joseph." He glanced at the small boy. "Ahhh, Joseph, where did you get that? You know you are not to have anything that would remind you of home." He walked to Joseph's cage, reached through the bars, and snatched away the bear. Then he walked back around the crates.

Peachy was not the type of boy to feel sorry for himself . . . even if he did feel blood dripping from his cut wrists. But he was angry—angry that someone would treat other human beings, especially children, like this. Yet what could he do about it? He forced himself to channel his anger into thinking of a way out. The rusted iron back of a dome-shaped object opened toward them.

"The boiler," he whispered. "It must be through there. If only they catch on in time."

"What?" Clair asked. "What did you say?"

Ahmed Bashir returned to the center of the cages. This time he was accompanied by the dark bloke Peachy had seen in the basement and one other taller, lighter-skinned man. "With your permission, Omar Rahman," Ahmed said to the third kidnapper. He received a curt nod in return. "Now," Ahmed Bashir shouted, "we move!"

•••

Danny led Inspector Avery through the lobby of the Palace Hotel. They were stopped by the desk clerk, who ran quickly around his counter when they came in. "Can I help you, sir?"

Avery flipped open his Scotland Yard identification. As he continued to walk, he snapped his fingers at a bobby trailing along behind. "Arrest him," he said simply. The stunned clerk was led away, babbling.

Danny took the policeman to the doorway leading to the stairs. "This is the way to the basement." The two descended the long flight of steps toward the warmth and soapy smells of the laundry.

Halfway down, Avery halted and motioned for silence. For the remainder of the journey they walked as softly as they could, stopping every time a board squeaked or a timber groaned. They proceeded only when the chamber below continued silent and still.

Avery led the way around the last corner as Danny pointed out the location of the hidden room. Immediately the boy noticed that the heap of tattered linen that had once blocked the hidden room was now pushed completely aside, as if someone had already gone that way.

"We may be too late," Danny said in a worried tone. "They could

have already gotten out." Avery started to respond when there was a noise from inside the dark room. The inspector held his finger to his lips again and slowly moved toward the room.

Suddenly a figure jumped from behind the door. By reflex, Avery swung his heavy cane at the man. Before he could connect, though, it was knocked from his hand.

Avery followed the arc of the stick with a swing of his left fist up from his waist. The solid blow landed squarely on the chest of the other and sent the man sprawling to the floor.

It was then that a second shape emerged from the shadows. The second man was even bulkier than the first and moved clumsily.

Danny shouted, "Look out!" to Inspector Avery. Then he flung himself at the second man's legs.

The flying tackle carried Danny and his target across the floor and into the row of tile that decorated the bricks.

"Ow, Danny," said Duff's voice. "What'd you do that for? Don't play so rough. I don't like it."

"Duff?" Danny asked with amazement. "Is that you?"

"Quite right, Wiggins," said the muffled voice of Sherlock Holmes from the tangle on the floor that was the detective struggling with the police inspector.

"Mr. Holmes?" queried a bewildered Avery. "Where are you?"

"Right before your eyes!" Holmes said as he pulled a mask from his face.

Danny sighed with relief and allowed his arm to relax, letting his grip loosen from Duff's neck.

"I will say this, Mr. Holmes," Avery said, wiping the sweat from his forehead with a soft white handkerchief. "You do like dramatic entrances, don't you? Because of that disguise, I nearly killed you."

"Yes, Inspector Avery." Holmes chuckled. "And were it not that I am me, I might have died."

Avery's features bunched up in confusion at the comment.

Danny turned to look at his friend but saw the features and dress of an old sailor.

"Duff! You're in disguise, too! What's going on here?"

"Very quickly," Holmes said. "More explanations later. I employed Mr. Bernard earlier today. We had to tackle you both because you might have been Omar Rahman's accomplices."

"But what is it you've come here for," Inspector Avery asked peevishly, "so far away from the action? Anyone can see that this is a dead end."

"Tell me, Inspector, when you track a rabbit to its hole, do you not have another hunter at the other exits from its warren so it cannot escape? To put it quite simply, Inspector, this is the other path to the den, and assuming there took place the inevitable . . . the . . . ahhh . . . the *usual* . . . police work at the other end, we'll soon be stewing our hare."

Holmes led them to the abandoned boiler. "If I am correct, sir, our rabbit will first show its ears right here."

"Down here?" Avery pointed to a tiny grate in the floor. "No one could get through that!"

"No, no, Inspector, use your head," Holmes said. "In any case, if we could run in now using full force, the first thing they would do is grab the closest child to use as a hostage. That closest one could be your daughter. No, we must wait for them to come to us, quietly picking them off one at a time."

•••

Peachy and Clair were the last in the line of six children being herded along by the dark-skinned man. Clair whispered that his name was Abdul Gaafar. They were taken around the crates and brought face-to-face with the boiler.

"So that's really where it is," he murmured. "The boiler is the passageway into the next room. How did Danny and I miss it?"

Gaafar climbed inside the metal chamber and fiddled with a series of latches that had kept the door securely fastened from the inside.

"That's it," Peachy said.

"No talking!" demanded Bashir. He poked a small but wicked-looking revolver into Peachy's side. "You will be silent!"

•••

Danny heard the rattling noises first and jumped away from where he leaned on the wheel-like handle of the boiler. "Mr. Holmes!" he called in a hoarse whisper. "They're coming from inside the boiler!"

"Yes, my boy, I know. Hide somewhere and be ready to fight if necessary."

"You knew?" Avery asked in disbelief. "Then why did you not share your knowledge with the rest of us?"

"Simply for the reason that I feared the waiting might make you do something foolish like rushing in."

Sherlock Holmes cut his explanation short when the sound of the final latch being thrown echoed from within the steel cylinder. He and the inspector took up positions on the sides of the tank, waiting for the next move of the criminals. Holmes pointed to the stout cane Avery carried and made a smashing motion into the palm of his hand. Avery nodded.

The wheel of the boiler revolved slowly as if a ghost were spinning it around. The rusty hinges on the large metal hatch creaked loudly as the door was slowly swung open.

A dark-skinned man poked his head out into the room. He stared at the floor as he stepped out of the belly of the metal chamber.

Just then Avery swing the heavy knobbed walking stick into the back of the man's skull. The kidnapper dropped without a sound into the waiting arms of Sherlock Holmes, who dragged the limp body aside and motioned for Danny to take his place beside the exit.

The next person out was the tiny figure of Joseph, who Danny recognized from his likeness in the papers as the first boy kidnapped. Danny reached out and grabbed him, covering the child's mouth so he couldn't scream, but Joseph didn't even try. He seemed numb.

When the little boy finally looked up at Danny, his eyes widened. *You're not a kidnapper!* his eyes seemed to say. He smiled and nodded. At Danny's gesture, he sat down quietly out of the way.

Three more children came out, each handled the same way,

before Clair emerged. She saw Danny, and he did not need to grab her. She ran to him and hugged him, then ran to her father. Both Averys were crying softly, so Holmes sent them aside and motioned for Duff to take Avery's place.

But the next figure through the opening was not who was expected. Instead of Peachy, the photographer emerged from the black hole.

Startled, Danny made a grab for the man and missed.

The photographer, now known to them as Ahmed Bashir, shouted a warning and fired a shot that ricocheted off a pipe and whined away in the darkness.

"Grab him, Duff!" Danny yelled.

Danny flung himself onto the gun arm and wrestled to keep the revolver pointed toward the floor.

Bashir squeezed the trigger again. The round exploded into the metal of the boiler like the blow of a hammer.

Danny was losing the struggle for the gun when he saw a pair of large hands appear around Bashir's throat.

"You are not nice," Duff said loudly. "I don't like not nice." He picked the kidnapper up so suddenly and forcefully that the man's head smashed into the top of the tank.

Bashir dropped his weapon and crumpled to the pavement.

"Quick now!" Holmes urged Danny. "The inspector and Duff will stay here. We must save Peachy and catch their leader, or this may happen all over again!"

Back on the other side of the boiler, Danny discovered Peachy. His friend had again been knocked unconscious.

The leader ran down a long corridor. Holmes and Danny quickly followed.

Danny guessed that the corridor must be the one that connected to the lift under the photographer's shop.

By the time Holmes and Danny reached it, the leader had already started the lift and was inside and on his way up.

"Stand back," the kidnapper leader ordered, brandishing a brown glass bottle, "unless you want this acid in your face!" Danny heard the leader snicker as he traveled to safety.

Underneath the platform was the mechanism that worked the lift.

"Quick, Wiggins!" Holmes said. "No time to lose. Do you see how much space there is next to the motor? Good! Now crawl under there and yank out the wires!"

Immediately Danny understood. Giving no thought to what could happen to him, he dove into the machinery. Reaching up with one hand, he pulled a wire from the electric motor and it stopped.

Danny covered his head as the drum began to wind the other way, slowly at first, then gradually gaining speed. Then all at once it stopped, touching down on its base just over his head. Through the metal floor above him, he heard the muffled voice of Sherlock Holmes.

"I must thank your accomplice for the use of his pistol," Holmes said. "Believe me, Omar Rahman, I am an excellent shot. If you wish to throw your bottle at me while I throw a bullet at you, please continue. Otherwise, set it down very carefully and step out of the lift."

A moment later Danny heard Holmes again. "All right now, Wiggins. You may reconnect the wire." When the cable was attached again, the floor slowly began to rise.

When there was enough room to crawl out from underneath, Danny saw Holmes holding a sullen Rahman at gunpoint. To Danny's relief, he also saw Peachy looking on, rubbing his head. The elevator platform was sent on its way to the street level above. Soon it would be filled with policemen riding it back down.

Epilogue

The Baker Street Brigade, along with Clair and Inspector Avery, gathered at their headquarters at 221B to discuss the events that had transpired the day before. Sherlock Holmes sat in his thick comfortable chair by the small fireplace, smoking a disreputable long-stemmed clay pipe, which filled the air with a smelly gray mist.

"Why were we targeted, Mr. Holmes?" Inspector Avery asked. "What did I ever do to the Mahdists?"

"Well, Avery," Holmes said, "you held a position of authority in Her Majesty's forces. You, Caravaldi, and the others were responsible for army actions against the slavers—actions that led to many executions."

"So are the kidnappers related to the ones executed?" Danny asked.

"Cousins, yes. More closely though, Omar Rahman, the leader, is the brother of Abu Mohammed Rahman, one of the . . ."

"Slavers," Avery finished. "One of the Sudanese slave traders executed by General Gordon as an example. My company and I were the ones who captured him. Things are beginning to fit into place now."

"But that doesn't explain where the hotel connection comes in," Peachy said.

"Ahhh, but it does," Holmes exclaimed. "Omar Rahman was educated in America. With his speech, manners, and the wealth of the Mahdist conquerors behind him, he was able to acquire the ownership of the Palace Hotel. Like our friend, Bashir, the photographer, he posed as a Turk. He was very well treated and even liked in this country. The rest of the story is obvious."

"Except one detail," Clair said. "The man with yellow hands that the Caravaldis' nanny described . . . who is he? Which is he?"

"The man with the yellow-stained hands, Clair," Holmes said, "is none other than Bashir, the photographer. I didn't realize this myself until Danny mentioned to me that the smell of sulfuric acid in my lab reminded him of the photographer's shop he had visited and the photographer who had taken your picture and was so nervous about the boys being in his place of business that he paid them to leave. The acid is used in depositing the silver on the photographic plates, but it also stains skin yellow."

"Is that why he wore gloves?" Inspector Avery asked.

"Indeed. Once the nanny's description was published in the papers, he realized he would be a suspect unless he hid his hands somehow, but the staining doesn't just wash away. It has to wear off as the body sheds old layers of skin. Gloves were his only alternative."

"Why in the world would he have put himself at risk beforehand by taking a picture of Clair in front of my very house?" Avery asked.

"I believe you have answered your own question, Inspector. Bashir could not always participate in the actual kidnapping, so there had to be a way for his accomplice, Gaafar, to be certain they had the right child. Hence the photographs. If you look into the activities of all the children approximately one week before their disappearances, you will find they all had photos taken."

"Amazing!" Avery exclaimed. "Absolutely amazing! I am so

very grateful to you, Mr. Holmes. If it weren't for you, my daughter would have been—" he paused—"er, what would have become of her, Mr. Holmes?"

Holmes's expression became grim. He spoke slowly and clearly. "Inspector Avery, your daughter and all the children involved would have been taken to Africa and sold into slavery. That was the revenge hidden behind the 'modest demands.'"

The group sank into deep thought at the prospect. Avery's jaw dropped. Gazing at the floor, Peachy ran his fingers through his hair and to his neck. "And you can imagine," Holmes continued, "the years ahead of them . . . a fate worse than death."

There was a knock at the door. "Ha!" Holmes snorted. "That will be the rest of the good news arriving. I took the liberty of sending our assistant, Duff."

Danny and Peachy exchanged a look. What was Duff involved in now?

The question was answered when Duff himself opened the door, accompanying the grinning, cigar-smoking Cap'n Mewsley.

"Just like Tel el Kebir," Mewsley was saying, "where I had to shoot four cannons all by myself!"

Words to Know

B

blackguard—a villain

Black Maria—police wagon for hauling prisoners

blimey—an expression of surprise or amazement

bloke—a fellow, a man

bowler—type of hat

Bristol fashion—clean and neat

burk—to strangle

C

chandlery—store dealing in supplies for ships

chap—a fellow, a man

civvies—civilians

copper—coin or spare change

cor—an expression of surprise

costermonger—street vendor dealing in vegetables

crusher—policeman

D

dab—clever

digs—lodgings

dipping—picking pockets

dodgy—suspicious

dotty—crazy

E

Embankment—spot on the river Thames, reinforced with a
   wall, making the water deeper

F

fishmonger—street vendor dealing in fish

flats—apartments

G

gammon—nonsense

good Queen Bess—Queen Elizabeth I

grotty—dirty, bad, or spoiled

H

hansom cab—two-wheeled carriage hired as transport

hieroglyphics—ancient Egyptian writing

K

kippers—smoked fish eaten for breakfast

L

lift—an elevator

M

mate—a friend

monograph—a paper on a scientific subject

N

nipper—small child

O

obelisk—upright pointed stone monument

oy—a word to get someone's attention, like "Hey!"

P

palaver—meaningless speech

Pasteur, Louis—scientist who discovered a cure
for rabies in 1885

peeler—policeman

pence—a penny

prog—food

pulling—picking pockets

R

righto—expression of agreement

rotter—a scoundrel

rum—foolish

S

scupper—to defeat or stop

sheet it home sudden—to finish quickly

shilling—coin equal to twelve pence

spooney—acting silly because of love

sprats—children

stone—measurement of weight

swell—well-dressed gentleman

T

tanning yard—where hides and furs are traded after they are
taken off the animal

too right—an expression of agreement

DID YOU KNOW . . . ?

Anthony Ashley Cooper, seventh Earl of Shaftesbury (mentioned in chapter 1 of this book), was real. He was a selfless worker for the children of London and a powerful believer in the Lord Jesus. It is a privilege for the authors of *The Mystery of the Yellow Hands* to be able to honor him by making him a character in this work of fiction.

Want more?

Go to thoenebooks.com and click on The Baker Street Detectives for fascinating info, questions to stir your heart, mind, and imagination, and much, much more.

About the Authors

Brothers **Jake and Luke Thoene** have long loved Sherlock Holmes, mysteries, and the city of London—all important elements for the Baker Street Detectives series. Both attended university in London, training in film and audio productions. They have collaborated on nine novels in three different series, among them: *Mystery Lights of Navajo Mesa* and *Legend of the Desert Bigfoot* in the Last Chance Detectives series and *The Mystery of the Yellow Hands*, *The Giant Rat of Sumatra*, *The Jeweled Peacock of Persia*, and *The Thundering Underground* in the Baker Street Detectives series. They also wrote the screenplay for *The Last Chance Detectives* (Tyndale and Focus on the Family) when Jake was twenty years old and Luke only seventeen.

Jake Thoene has climbed onto the CBA best-sellers list with the titles of his timely Chapter 16 series: *Shaiton's Fire*, *Firefly Blue*, and *Fuel the Fire*. His research on domestic counterterrorism included hand-to-hand and small-arms training. His books are gutsy and realistic, foretelling the many challenges and threats that face America.

Jake teaches and researches on the West Coast, where he, his wife, Wendi, and their three sons live.

Luke Thoene has also continued the Thoene family legacy of writing. In the exciting Legends of Valor series—*Sons of Valor, Brothers of Valor*, and *Fathers of Valor*—Luke traces the upheavals and events of the nineteenth century through the experiences of the Sutton family and their descendants. He also produces the Thoene family audiobooks. Luke lives on California's central coast.

For more information about Jake, Luke, and other Thoene family titles:
jakethoene.com
thoenebooks.com
familyaudiolibrary.com

THOENE FAMILY CLASSICS™

✪ ✪ ✪

THOENE FAMILY CLASSIC HISTORICALS
by Bodie and Brock Thoene

Gold Medallion Winners*

THE ZION COVENANT
Vienna Prelude*
Prague Counterpoint
Munich Signature
Jerusalem Interlude
Danzig Passage
Warsaw Requiem*
London Refrain
Paris Encore
Dunkirk Crescendo

THE ZION CHRONICLES
The Gates of Zion*
A Daughter of Zion
The Return to Zion
A Light in Zion
The Key to Zion*

THE SHILOH LEGACY
In My Father's House*
A Thousand Shall Fall
Say to This Mountain

SHILOH AUTUMN

THE GALWAY CHRONICLES
Only the River Runs Free*
Of Men and of Angels
Ashes of Remembrance*
All Rivers to the Sea

THE ZION LEGACY
Jerusalem Vigil
Thunder from Jerusalem
Jerusalem's Heart
Jerusalem Scrolls
Stones of Jerusalem
Jerusalem's Hope

A.D. CHRONICLES
First Light
Second Touch
Third Watch
Fourth Dawn
Fifth Seal
and more to come!